Fly Me to the MOON

BEV ELLE

Bev Elle Press

Fly Me to the Moon

Copyright © 2015 by Bev Elle

Editing by Rare Bird Editing www.rarebirdediting.com

Book design by Amy Queau of QDesign

bevelleauthor@gmail.com

This book is a work of fiction. The names, characters, places and incidents are products of the writer's imagination or have been used fictitiously and are not to be construed as real. Any resemblance to persons, living or dead, actual events, locale or organizations is entirely coincidental.

Printed in the United States of America by Bev Elle Press

Publisher's Cataloging-in-Publication data
Elle, Bev.
Fly Me to the Moon / Bev Elle
ISBN—13: 978-0692384725
ISBN—10: 0692384723
1. Romance —Suspense — Interracial/Multicultural. 2. Category — Subcategory. 3. More categories —Modifiers. I. Elle, Bev. II. Fly Me to the Moon
First Edition: February 2015
14 13 12 11 10 / 10 9 8 7 6 5 4 3 2 1

FLY ME TO THE MOON

≪ Chapter 1 ≫

Jessamy heard the resonant whistling of the old Frank Sinatra classic at the same time her co-worker warned her that the carrier of the tune was coming their way.

"WG incoming," Susan whispered *sotto voce*. Jessamy cringed internally every time her co-workers called him WG, an acronym for Weird Griffin. He had a medical condition much like her own— but she'd sought help—something he'd been unwilling to do. Regardless, it wasn't like he could stifle his weirdness without behavior therapy and psychotropic medications. Jessamy understood this.

Among her co-workers, Jessamy was the only one who knew that Dr. Griffin Sanderson was a brilliant man who was also very kind and generous. She alone also knew that beneath the out-of-season corduroys and white button-downs he usually wore, there was a hard, muscular body inside. Because like so many other routines he was obsessive about, exercise was part of his daily regimen. And she had benefitted from it. Once upon a time.

Before she'd learned of his peculiarities, Jessamy had considered Griffin a fine specimen. He wasn't just handsome; he seemed to have been created with a special mold that had been tossed once he was fully formed so no other mortal could possess his extraordinary good looks. From a distance she took note of his inky black hair, intensely expressive blue eyes and that banging body hidden inside . . . Surprise, surprise Griffin was wearing linen slacks, and conspicuously absent were those black-framed, pseudo-hipster, geeky glasses he usually wore! She tore her eyes away from checking out her neighbor and greeted her next customer.

Everyone working the ticket counter was suddenly busy, although they knew WG would hone in as if he were a homing pigeon and Jessamy Taylor was his natural place to roost. Each employee of

East West Airlines had experienced the singular customer encounter that was Weird Griffin and never wanted to again if they could help it. Jessamy was the only ticket agent who could handle him, and she often wondered just what made her the recipient of such a dubious honor, besides the two years they'd dated.

Though several other counters had shorter lines, Griffin fell in behind the twenty or so people in Jessamy and Susan's line.

"Like clockwork," Susan said as she weighed their current customer's luggage.

"This is the third Wednesday of the month. He's headed to Miami to irradiate the citizenry of greater Miami-Dade County in need of oncological services," Jessamy said.

"You seem to know a lot about what he does," Susan said. "Don't tell me you've gotten soft where WG is concerned."

Jessamy blushed in spite of herself, and tried to act as if Susan Hale, her bestie at work hadn't touched a nerve. "He's not so bad." *Especially if you're not in a relationship with him and having to put up with his rituals.*

"He puts you through your paces on a weekly basis." Susan snorted. "No one should have to sanitize before handling a customer's boarding pass."

"I really don't mind that at all," Jessamy said. "Besides, it's rote now, I've been doing it so long."

"This is why we all happily let you have him. If I didn't know any better, your reaction just now would lead one to believe there's something between you and the good doctor."

She wanted to deny it, emphatically, but Jessamy had never been any good at lying. She sighed. "Ancient history."

"How ancient?"

"Ended two years ago."

Susan was downright giddy. "And how did we not know about this fling, especially me?"

Jessamy half-resented Susan's referral to hers and Griffin's relationship as a fling, because Griffin never considered it as such, nor did she, but she wouldn't mince words. Jessamy relived their past in a few seconds each and every time she and Griffin came into contact in some version or another. She wondered if he did the same thing, but

Griffin was always so polite and professional with her now, she couldn't tell.

"*You* didn't know about it for the same reason *we* never know who I'm dating. I'd just left flight service and taken the position here when it ended."

"So what's the story?"

"We met when I moved back to Tallahassee from Atlanta."

"You moved here when your father got sick, right?" Susan said.

"You're all set," Jessamy said to her customer, and handed him his boarding pass and luggage claim receipt. Her smile was perfunctory as she motioned for the next customer to approach the counter.

"About a year after I moved onto Griffin's cul-de-sac near Golden Eagle, we began to date."

"Nice neighborhood," Susan said. "Hey, how can you afford that on a ticket agent's salary?"

"I was a flight attendant then, remember? With a roommate. Anyway, now my mother lives with me."

"Oh yeah," Susan said. "A second income helps when you're paying for pricey real estate."

"Tell me about it," Jessamy said, and then called to the next person in line who was preoccupied with a cell phone. "May I help who's next?"

"Couldn't you tell right away there was something off about him?"

"Maybe. But I saw potential. He rescued me from an exploding garbage bag full of magazines and junk mail on my driveway the first day I moved in. He was wearing corduroys in ninety degree heat, a faded Star Wars tee-shirt, and latex gloves even then. I should've gotten a clue."

"We rarely react appropriately to red flags," Susan said. "If I did, I wouldn't be on husband number three." She frowned and weighed in another bag. Susan and Jessamy were an efficient team. They'd processed six customers within a few minutes.

Jessamy laughed. "I know, right?" Then she began checking in customer number seven. "Thank you for flying East-West."

"I'm still waiting to hear what you saw in WG, despite his obvious deficit in the weird vs. normal ratio," Susan said as Jessamy's fingers flew over the keyboard. Jessamy swallowed her guilt at hearing the WG acronym, yet again.

"Well, he was quite charming in a geeky, hot professor sort of way. Like Clark Kent without the phone booth. Except what he lacked in super powers, he made up for with his bulging IQ. Then I found out he treated my dad, and I saw a side of him that was so caring and compassionate. But he avoided me for a whole year, because he thought it might be unethical. My dad changed doctors to put him out of his misery." Griffin had been more than competent in all areas of courtship, even in the bedroom when he wasn't succumbing to one of his many quirks after sex, but she wasn't about to share that with Susan Hale.

Susan barked a short laugh. "Smart is sexy. Compassionate is sexy. Weird isn't. How did you put up with his crazy, given your own OCD?"

"I understood it, I suppose. To a point." Jessamy glared at her. "And just so you know, people with OCD are not crazy."

"Sorry," Susan said with a sheepish frown, but Jessamy's gentle upbraiding did not deter her from further inquisition. "Something else about him had to make you stick around for two years, though." Susan leaned in and whispered. "He must be hung."

"Susan!"

"Well?"

Jessamy winced. "I am not about to have an anatomy discussion in the workplace with you."

"You're no fun."

"I told you, my life, even when I was a flight attendant, wasn't as glamorous as many suspect."

"Well, wow me with how boring you and he were as a couple then."

"He dated me like an old-school suitor. He always brought wine, flowers, or some small gift when he came over for dinner. My favorite was a hardback collection of The *Song of Ice and Fire* Books to include *A Dance with Dragons*."

"Sounds like a keeper to me. What made it go sour?"

"Ever watch that show, The Big Bang Theory?"

"When it's on re-runs sometimes."

"Well, he's like a cross between Leonard and Sheldon, complete with the most irritating of their idiosyncrasies."

"Wow! That's quite a personality to deal with."

"Yeah, and especially if a girl has some of those tendencies herself. It's enough to deal with all the rules in my own home, but then to have to multiply that times ten and have to deal in another house."

"Mindboggling. But if he was as sweet as you say, couldn't you overlook his cra— uh eccentricities?"

"Believe me, I tried. It just seemed to get worse rather than better, and the last six months we argued all the time over what for most couples would seem inconsequential, but his refusal to get help was what sealed it."

"You'd think a guy as smart as he is would get that."

"That's just the point. He knew too much about the drugs and their possible side effects. The man has a fundamental resistance to any drug other than the occasional aspirin and antibiotics."

"Bummer," Susan said, just as the subject of their conversation became the next in line after the customer they were checking in.

As Griffin approached her at the counter, Jessamy rubbed antibacterial hand sanitizer liberally onto her hands, put on her most professional smile, and greeted him. This somehow comforted her as a fellow germophobe. Jessamy just hid hers well enough from friends not to be dubbed weird.

"Dr. Sanderson."

"Ms. Taylor."

They were so formal each time they interacted during his travels, no one would ever have guessed they lived on the same street and had known one another five years. Case in point with Susan.

Griffin handed her his boarding pass, printed out and meticulously trimmed to regulation size. It looked as if it had come from the airline's printer. She had told Griffin on more than one occasion that he could even use his smartphone to present his boarding pass, but he preferred to go old school. She couldn't blame him. There was something reassuring about having the document in hand.

"Let me guess," Jessamy began with a smirk, "You're off to Miami."

"I can't imagine how you came to that conclusion," Griffin said with that almost-grin he sported in mixed company.

"Oh, a little birdie told me," she said as she checked him in. "What's new in the world of radiation oncology?"

Griffin's eyes lit up. "Intraoperative radiotherapy."

"So, no more external delivery?"

"Maybe further down the road," he said. "Miami is on board with it for some patients. I'm hoping to get Tallahassee General on board, soon."

"If anyone can convince, them, I'm certain it'll be you."

"You have such confidence in my power of persuasion," he said. There were flirtatious undertones to the way he interacted with her this time, and Jessamy remembered something was different about Griffin besides new clothes.

"Hey, you're wearing contacts," she blurted. Gone were the Clark Kentish-glasses that usually covered his prismatic blue eyes. The unique color was enhanced without the distortion of the bigger lenses.

He grinned. "Yeah. I figured it was time I retired the glasses."

Jessamy actually stared at him then, because something transpired between them that she'd never felt before. She thought it snagged him, too, because whatever it was caused their eyes to lock and neither of them could look away for a long moment, but then his eyes darted away.

She didn't bother asking him if he had luggage to check. He always carried on because the one time he'd checked baggage since nine eleven had been a disaster. A random TSA check had sent him into a near apoplectic state. Of course, the letter he carried on his person from his personal physician, which East West also had a copy of, is the only thing that saved him from being arrested and removed bodily from the airport. This and many minor incidents with other East West employees had earned him his unpleasant moniker.

"You're all set," Jessamy said, presenting her professional smile again.

Griffin's affect returned to being as flat as it usually was, but Jessamy could see the hint of a smile at one corner of his mouth, and only because she knew him well enough to recognize it. He hesitated, but then ended their exchange with a terse, "Thank you, Ms. Taylor."

"You're welcome, Dr. Sanderson."

Now came her favorite part of their weekly interactions. Him walking away. Jessamy reveled in the fact she was the only one at the counter who could vividly recall the perfection of the ass cheeks that were only hinted at by the hang of his linen trousers. It was ninety-five degrees outside so the linen was a great choice, but then she also remembered. He went commando. She clenched her thighs together as if to ward off any reaction on her part that resembled sexual attraction, and slathered her hands with sanitizer to prepare for her next customer. Been there. Done that. Too unhinged to keep the wookie tee shirt.

Before Griffin turned the corner and was out of sight, he did something that was totally uncharacteristic of his usual routine: he turned, looked back, and waited just long enough for her eyes to meet his again before he rounded the corner wheeling his luggage behind him.

Susan followed where Jessamy's eyes were trained. "Too bad he gives off such an unavailable vibe. He's really not that bad looking underneath all the corduroy and his penchant for pocket protectors."

If only you knew. Jessamy fanned herself with a handy brochure on the counter.

"WG's got your motor running," Susan teased. "How long's it been since you've been on a date with a man who doesn't wear suspenders and bowties?"

Sure, some of Griffin's fashion choices were ill-advised, but he was so much more than the clothes he wore.

Susan used Jessamy's silence as an opportunity to answer her own question. "Not since Captain Manwhore. Am I right?"

"Don't remind me," Jessamy said. "The prick."

"Strong words coming from you, my friend. WG is obviously one you could put in the same category since you two aren't together anymore."

"Well, not exactly," Jessamy hedged. "To his credit, Griffin was never a prick. He just lacked the ability to relate to me like a normal man, given his extreme obsessive compulsive disorder."

Susan slid more weighed luggage out to its owner with a smile, then turned back to Jessamy. "How so?"

"That's for me to know and you to find out. I'm done sharing my sordid past with you. Besides if I told you, I'd have to hunt you down like a hit man and snuff you out in your sleep." Jessamy, said so only Susan could hear, and then smiled at the next passenger and began to check her in.

Susan laughed a big cackling laugh that had the few customers left in their lines giving her the side-eye.

Jessamy's face grew warm and she busied herself on the monitor to see how many passengers they had yet to check in on the currently boarding flights. But her mind was still on the quirky Dr. Sanderson and his superior physical assets. She hated when she wasn't attached to anyone. Her libido went into overdrive and she had lascivious thoughts about her neighbor with whom she'd learned the hard way she was not compatible.

Oh my God, I got busted ogling Griffin Sanderson's ass, and spilled my guts to Susan "The Mouth" Hale!

Jessamy knew then without a doubt. She needed to get laid.

≪ Chapter 2 ≫

Kyla peered into the refrigerator as if it were her own as Jessamy chopped vegetables for a salad. "Why don't you have any yogurt?" Had it been anyone else, Jessamy might have been peeved that Kyla opened her fridge without asking, and then made requests for items which clearly weren't in there. It was, of course, organized by product type and height, just like her pantry and her cupboards, and Kyla knew this and honored her system.

Jessamy gave her a side-long glance. "I need to go grocery shopping, but I didn't call you over to discuss the contents of my refrigerator. Grab your choice of salad dressing while you're in there."

"I'm hungry now. That casserole you've got in the oven is going to take a minute." Kyla selected Balsamic Vinaigrette and set it on the island.

Jessamy filled two bowls with the veggies and handed one to Kyla. "Here. Have a salad until the casserole gets done. We'll eat our meal in stages like the French."

Kyla scrunched up her nose as if she were smelling something distasteful, but didn't refuse the salad. She straddled the barstool, brought her legs together once she'd cleared the top of it, and dug in. While Jessamy sat demurely and adjusted her place setting until it was just right. Placemat, silverware and a folded napkin, fully symmetrical, before she began to eat.

Kyla poured them both a glass of wine, which they sipped leisurely after the salad was consumed, and waited the last few minutes for their main course.

"You know Rick keeps asking me to introduce him to one of my friends," Kyla said.

"Who's Rick again?"

"My friend at the firm who just moved here from Miami."

"I think we're too old for blind dates," Jessamy said.

Kyla took a huge, inelegant gulp of her wine and topped them off again. "Speak for yourself."

"We're twenty-nine, Ky."

"Tell me something I don't know."

The oven buzzer went off and Jessamy sprung up from her bar stool to retrieve the chicken tetrazzini from the oven. Donning oven mitts carefully, she pulled the casserole dish out and set it gingerly on a trivet on the island.

"That smells delicious," Kyla said licking her lips.

"Thanks." Jessamy smiled. Gracious hostess that she was, she took the spatula and cut a generous portion and served her friend first, then herself. Retaking her seat next to Kyla, she didn't immediately begin because she didn't want to burn the top of her mouth with the melted cheese, but Kyla took no such precaution. She dug in, blowing the small forkful she ventured to eat several times before hazarding to try it. It still burned, because Kyla immediately drank another sip of wine.

"Slow down," Jessamy said. "I promise not to take your food back if you don't scarf it down in five minutes flat."

"I only had a Snickers bar for lunch," Kyla said. "I was working on a deadline all day."

"Why didn't you call for delivery?"

"I got caught up writing briefs for this case I'm working on, and there were no paralegals or secretaries available to help me. Everyone else is working on class-action suits.

"I love my job, but even I stop to eat, and you should, too. What good will you be to your firm passed out on the floor with low blood sugar?"

"That's rather unlikely. As long as there are vending machines, I can always get some high fructose corn syrup-infused delicious treat to tide me over."

Jessamy frowned. "If you don't eat better you're going to die an untimely death."

Kyla grinned. "But I'll be happy." She took another bite of tetrazzini and didn't wait to finish chewing before she started talking again. "So, what can I tell you about Rick Traynor?"

"That his real name isn't Rick?"

"I'm serious. He's a great guy."

"And you would know this because? I mean, I thought he just came to work at your firm."

"Well, he did, but we went to undergrad and law school together."

Jessamy narrowed her eyes. "Were you and Rick ever . . .?"

"We went out for a while in Law School."

"Which means you slept with him." Jessamy stood and began to pace. "Why do you think I'd want a guy you used to do?"

"Because I never 'did' him, and he really is a great guy."

"If he's so great why'd you break it off with him? And why'd you never 'do him?'"

"Contrary to popular opinion, I didn't sleep with every guy I've ever dated. We weren't up for anything serious at the time. I'd totally 'do him' now, but I love Carter, and last I checked he wasn't into doing a ménage."

"You are so full of it, Kyla. While I'm flattered you'd like to hook me up with your leavings, I don't think I'll take you up on that." Jessamy took her seat and tucked into her own meal.

"It's your loss. Rick's a great lay from what I hear through the rumor mill."

"You did not just say that."

"What? Well, that's what they say."

"Then you date him again. I'd rather not date a guy who has that kind of reputation. Thank you very much."

"I'll remember that as I continue to moonlight as your matchmaker."

"I may just go through one of those dating services," Jessamy mused. "There's one that really goes the extra mile to match you with someone compatible."

"I don't know, Jess. You sure you want to put yourself out there like that? It smacks so much of desperation."

"I don't have the time or inclination to go out and find someone, especially with Mom being here with me, and all."

It was as if her mention of her mother conjured her up, because she entered the kitchen from the back door, asking, "What can't you do with Mom being here and all?"

Clarice Taylor was still a very attractive woman at almost sixty. Jessamy had inherited her caramel-colored skin and long wavy hair from somewhere deep in their part-Dominican lineage. Despite her COPD diagnosis a few months after Jessamy's father passed, Clarice was doing reasonably well. She had been outfitted with a portable oxygen tank six months before and Jessamy had insisted she move in with her since she wasn't romantically attached and it didn't seem as if it was going to happen soon. It had put a kink in her dating life, which had already been suffering due to inattention and disinterest. Because the last couple of relationships had bombed terribly. Jessamy was beginning to think she was too set in her ways to ever find the right man.

Her mother's comment made Jessamy feel as if she'd been caught with her hand in the cookie jar. She did not want her mother to feel as if she were inhibiting her sex life, or her ability to find a husband, which had been one of Clarice's main concerns about moving in.

"Nothing at all," Jessamy said. "I was just making an excuse so Kyla wouldn't feel the necessity to set me up with one of her old boyfriends."

"Is that what you young people do nowadays? Swap exes?"

"No, Mrs. T," Kyla said. "I just tried to fix Jess up with one former boyfriend of mine. It's been so long since we dated, I wouldn't call him an ex anymore. And he'd be perfect for Jessamy."

"Are you still with . . .?" Clarice snapped a finger, "What's his name?"

"Carter?" Kyla nodded. "Yes and it's getting serious. Which is why I don't care if Jessamy dates Rick."

"The Steel Magnolias swear anyone named Mark, Rick or Steve are gay. You trying to set my daughter up with a man on the—what do they call it?—the down below?"

"It's down-low," Jessamy said. "And I don't think so Mama. Kyla has . . . intimate knowledge of his sexual preferences."

"Is that some kind of code that she's had carnal knowledge of this young man?" Clarice peered across the top of the glasses perched on her nose and glared at Ky.

"I'm saving myself for marriage," Kyla proclaimed, a swath of her natural curls falling across her forehead as she dug back into her Tetrazzini.

Jessamy laughed and reached into the cupboard to get a place setting for her mother. "Mama, have a seat, the casserole is still warm."

Clarice sat on the last empty barstool and adjusted the tiny oxygen tank at her side. "Maybe you should find a singles group at the Catholic Church like I found Bingo."

"I just might go with you," Jessamy said. "Are there any handsome single men at Bingo around our age?"

"The unattached men there are all older than me," Clarice said, as she put a small portion of the Tetrazzini on her plate and served herself some salad. "But if you're into that sort of thing."

"You can't blame a girl for asking," Jessamy said. "How was Bingo tonight, anyway?"

"It was fine. I even won a game."

"What'd you win?" Kyla asked before Jessamy could get another word in. She pushed the curls back from her eyes, opening up her face again, since the current topic of conversation was safer than the last one.

"Of all things, a back massager," Clarice said. She rummaged through her purse and pulled a long, narrow box out.

Kyla burst out laughing, and Jessamy scowled at her, but her lips twitched uncontrollably.

"You might want to let Jess borrow that, Mrs. T."

"What? Why?"

"Mama," Jessamy said. "It's a vibrator."

Clarice dropped the box like the contents were hot, or might sting her, and it clattered onto the island. "Well, if that don't beat all. I wonder if the folks at the Catholic Church know what kind of prizes the Bingo folks are giving out over there."

"I'm sure the nuns think it's just a back massager, too, Mama," Jessamy said. "Eat your dinner. Maybe we can sell it on Craig's list." She said this knowing she'd likely keep it and just pay her mother for it. Then she cringed at the depths her love life had sunk to.

≪ Chapter 3 ≫

Later, when her mother had retired for the evening, and Jessamy took her nightly glass of wine on the screened-in deck out back, she wondered if her haste to sell the vibrator was indeed inadvisable. Since Kyla's friend at work turned out to be one of her exes, and a road down which Jessamy did not want to travel, she was prospectless once again. The vibrator might be just the ticket to get her deprived libido some action. She wondered why she'd never used a vibrator before when she spotted a shadowy figure at the edge of her back yard.

Her eyes flew to the screen door to make sure it was latched before she decided to go inside and get her mace when a familiar voice addressed her.

"Jessamy?"

What the heck was Griffin doing roaming out behind her house this time of night?

She placed a relieved hand on her chest, which heaved from fear, or the idea that Griffin had come up just after she'd thought about whether she should or shouldn't use a vibrator for the first time.

"What . . .?" She didn't get to finish her question before he answered it.

"I was hoping you were still a creature of habit and were having a nightcap around this time," he said as he approached the steps. "May I come in?"

She went to the screen door and unlatched it. "Sure, come on in."

To her surprise, his attire consisted of cargo shorts and a golf shirt, but she supposed he had to take off the cords, sweatpants and the button downs at some point. This however, was new. She gestured to one of the deck chairs and he took the one matching hers, separated by a small table where her wine glass and bottle sat. Griffin's cologne, a woodsy mixture underlined by sandalwood, drifted toward her. The same one she'd inhaled frequently when they'd been together. It was flagrantly sensual given her recent sexual drought.

Jessamy quickly put on her polite hostess persona, compliments of her good home training and former flight attendant experience. "Would you like a drink?"

"No, thank you. I don't think it would be good for me to drink with the medication I'm taking right now, especially since I have to get up early for work tomorrow." Just like Griffin to always overshare.

"Is this some new development?" She said, re-taking her seat again.

"You might say that," he answered. "Actually, it's what I wanted to talk to you about."

Jessamy nodded. "O—kay. . ."

"Remember when we stopped seeing each other, you said that if I were to get better, you would consider seeing me again." She looked at him, trying to see his eyes in the ambient light from the kitchen windows, but she had the lights off on the deck so as not to draw any bugs. She just imagined how earnest his eyes were at the moment. Jessamy was at a loss for words. It wasn't fair of him to spring this idea of reconciliation on her while she was in such dire need of male companionship.

"Wow, Griffin. Your timing is impeccable . . . but I'm seeing someone." Jessamy almost retracted the lie when Griffin stood and shifted into the light coming out of the kitchen window. The disappointment on his face made her want to give him another chance in the worst way. But the humiliation hadn't faded enough over time to travel that path again.

She couldn't stand the idea of him blowing chunks every time they made love, because that was exactly what happened. He reminded her of Billy Bob Thornton's character in the movie *Monster's Ball,* who vomited the first time he did the horizontal mambo with Halle Berry's character. Multiply that times every other encounter and she felt absolutely horrible a significant portion of the time they were intimate. That wreaked havoc on a girl's ego.

Besides, she wasn't totally being untruthful; Kyla did have a date for her, even if he was one of her previous flames, and Jessamy had turned him down just that evening. Any excuse to keep her from dealing with Griffin and his issues again, which made her issues pale in comparison, she had to take.

"Is it serious?" he asked.

Jessamy was so stunned by Griffin's proposition, she'd lost track of the conversation. "Is what serious?"

"Your relationship with this person you're . . . seeing." The tension in his voice could be misconstrued as jealousy, but it had been two years. Certainly, Griffin wasn't jealous. Things ended amicably between them despite all the arguing at the end.

"It's new, you know. I just want to see where it can go."

"Can't you just tell him you want to reconcile with your ex? He couldn't possibly know you as well as I do, or treat you any better than I can."

"I just can't with you, Griffin," she said. "You make me crazy, and the nausea and vomiting after sex—I had to go back into therapy to get over that. I don't want to be on that loony train again."

Griffin's countenance fell and he raised his hands as if in surrender. "Okay. Okay." He pushed open the screen door. "I'll see you at the terminal Wednesday night."

Jessamy locked the door behind him. She hadn't even acknowledged the progress she'd seen in him lately. Never had she been intentionally bitchy toward him, but something about traveling that road again made her irrational. She believed she'd done the right thing by turning him down. Yet, why did she feel gutted by the desire to run after him and apologize for being so short with him? When she moved to unlatch the door and call after him he disappeared around the corner from which he'd come.

"Pigs might fly today," Clarice exclaimed.

"Why's that?" Jessamy asked as she set their food offerings on one of the communal tables. The cul-de-sac was set up for food, activities and festively decorated for their annual block party.

"Griffin's here," her mother said.

Jessamy turned to see for herself. And there he was talking to their neighbors across the street, Mark and Jenny Fowler, who had two kids and a dog. When Griffin saw her and Clarice gawking, he waved.

Kyla walked up carrying a covered dish as they waved back. Jessamy had to rib her. "When are you going to get the message that you really don't live on this street anymore, chick?" Kyla had been her roommate before her mother moved in. Now she practically lived with Carter, but she had a condo that she was thinking of subletting.

"When you rat me out to the neighbors. I'm over here enough, they still don't know the difference, and they may grandfather me in because they love my cooking so much." She set the heavy Pyrex dish on the table and took it out of its quilted covering, leaving the aluminum foil on it to deter flies.

"You know you'd hate it if she weren't around," Clarice said. "Anyway, I invited some people from Bingo, so guests are welcome."

"I know, Mama. I just have to mess with Ky."

"Oh, I see them coming. Let me go show them where they can set their lawn chairs up in front of our house." Clarice took off in the direction of her friends where cars were being parked further down the street.

Kyla got a cup and filled it with ice from a cooler and then filled it with lemonade from a thermal jug. "Want one?" She asked Jessamy, gesturing to her cup.

"Sure."

She served her friend then looked leisurely around. "Looks like there's going to be a great turnout today." Then she almost choked on her lemonade, and Jessamy patted her on the back.

"Stop swallowing so fast. Do I always need to remind you to slow down when you're eating and drinking?"

She rasped, "I-Is that Griffin petting a dog over there?"

Jessamy shielded her eyes with her hand and peered across the cul-de-sac. If she'd seen it first, she might have choked on her lemonade, too. Griffin Sanderson was petting the Fowlers' dog. "Oh my God, he is!"

"Don't they have like a gazillion germs or something? And what happened to his glasses?"

"Actually, some would argue that dogs are cleaner than humans. And Griffin got contacts."

"Finally. You know, Jess, he's looking kind of good, today. You might want to tap that again since he's had a makeover and all."

Jessamy waved her off. "I couldn't possibly."

"Why not? The guy I see over there looks infinitely tappable." Kyla set her drink on the table and folded her arms.

Jessamy sipped her lemonade. "He may look tappable today, but you didn't have to experience what I did with him as his girlfriend for two years. I should've called it quits after our Christmas trip to the

Poconos, but I had fallen for him, and like so many misinformed women in history before me, I thought I could change him."

"You'd think you two would've been great together, twin OCD and all. And I thought you said the trip to the Poconos was perfect." Kyla said, air-quoting the word perfect.

"Everything was perfect up until that trip. We had so much in common. We both loved science fiction. We were both G.R.R. Martin geeks who watched the Game of Thrones show together and nitpicked how the show differed from the books. And even though I had the books on my kindle, he gifted me the hardbacks as a three-month anniversary present." Jessamy smiled at the memory.

"I remember. You two were enough to make regular folks gag."

"And you and Carter don't—with your copious PDA?"

Kyla laughed. "But at least we don't get all aroused over an episode of The Big Bang Theory."

"Carter likes that show."

"Not more than he likes me, though." Kyla actually twirled her hair.

"Is he coming today?"

"Yeah, after he does his Saturday morning nine holes with his boss. Ugh!"

"Good, we're going to need all the people we can get to eat up all this food." Jessamy eyed the tables balefully.

"Look!" Kyla said. "Griffin's holding the Fowlers' baby. Now doesn't that make your ovaries want to explode?"

Jessamy turned her head slowly, knowing the sight would slay her. Griffin *never* held babies. She took it all in as if in slow motion. Mark was holding their toddler in place as Jenny was cleaning up the sticky popsicle he was covered in, while Griffin was holding the four-month old. He cradled her a bit nervously at first, then he seemed to get his baby-holding legs under him and finally began to smile and talk to her.

Jessamy and Kyla could hear her baby giggle from where they stood. "Aww!" They said in tandem.

"Now that right there ought to earn a man another chance," Kyla said.

"I thought you were so eager to set me up with Rick," Jessamy said.

"Well, yeah, if you have no other prospects, but it looks like you have one right here under your nose."

"And this from the queen of been-there-done-that."

"I gave Carter a second chance, remember?"

"But that's different. You do not know the depth of humiliation I had to endure with Griffin, Ky."

Kyla pouted, looking hurt. "And I thought we told each other everything."

"Well, we do, but this is just so . . . personal." Jessamy's voice cracked.

Something in her friend's voice clued Kyla in that there might be something earth-shattering she didn't know about Jessamy's former relationship with Griffin.

"Come on. Let's take a bathroom break, have a real drink inside, something—and you tell me why you can't be with Griffin again."

As they walked the short expanse back to her house, Jessamy looked back and saw Griffin surreptitiously using his hand sanitizer before moving on to talk to the elderly couple at the next house. Some things never changed. But then some things did. This was the first time he'd actively participated in the block party. That in itself was a minor miracle.

"He did what?" Kyla said.

"Keep your voice down. You want Mama to come in here?"

Kyla paced. "I knew you guys had issues, but throwing up after sex? Geez, Jess. I'm so sorry. That would give *me* a complex and I'm fairly confident in myself."

"I could take his ritualistic demands and his odd requests for me to wash my hands or brush my teeth before kissing him sometimes, but it was the vomiting."

"All I've got to say, girl is, *Monster's Ball* much?"

Jessamy quailed. "Don't remind me. There's nothing like the sickening splash of your lover's stomach contents in the toilet bowl after sex."

"And he threw up every single time?"

"Well, to his credit, if we made love twice in one night there was only a bit of dry heaving afterward."

"And you still liked him enough not to run for the hills?"

"Yes. We'd been together six months, and I was falling for him. I had no way of knowing that his condition would kill my feelings for him in the long run."

"So, what? Did the vomiting just finally creep you out too much to stay?"

"It was sort of like that, I mean, I wanted a man who didn't have to practically wash his silverware and plates with hand sanitizer when we went to restaurants. One who didn't have to brush his teeth more than a half a dozen times a day, and insist I brush mine, too, especially before we kissed."

"Was there nothing that wasn't controlled with him?"

"Well, you know the orderliness and cleanliness I liked about him. A lot. It wasn't much different from how I like to keep house. It was just maddening trying to keep it all straight between two houses."

"You poor baby. Griffin overdosed you on OCD."

Jessamy laughed mirthlessly. "Yeah, there's a lot of truth in the adage that familiarity breeds contempt, because the better I got to know Griffin, the crazier he made me. The clincher was his refusal to try the meds. I finally had to call it quits."

"Yeah, Jess. You just go out with Rick next week. I'll go ahead and set that up." Kyla took a big gulp of wine, emptying her glass.

Jessamy followed suit. "So now you know."

"Oddly, I kind of wish I didn't know. I won't be able to look at him the same."

"Ky, you can't embarrass him like that. You have to act as if you don't know anything," Jessamy implored.

Kyla set her wine glass in the sink. "Okay, I'll be chill. I'll just probably throw up a little in my own mouth when I remember it."

Jessamy glared through narrowed eyes at Kyla.

"Okay, I'll have no response, physically or emotionally. I'll just feel sorry for him and for you—in my mind."

That was probably the extent of a promise she would get, so Jessamy took it.

≪ Chapter 4 ≫

The following week on Tuesday night found Jessamy on a date with Rick Traynor, Kyla's attorney friend, after all. She didn't want to be a liar and she figured she could go out with Rick a couple of times just to see if they had any chemistry whatsoever, and to see if she could overcome the idea that her best friend had once dated this guy on the regular.

Rick was considerably metrosexual in an I-was-once-an-asshat-frat-boy kind of way. Dirty blond hair sported an expensive haircut, and a flawlessly pressed designer suit covered his linebacker's frame. He insisted he'd just come from work and didn't have time to change, but he either wore his suits like a mannequin—stiff and unmoving all day—or he was trying his damnedest to impress her.

At least he wasn't a cheap date. They'd first taken in an early movie and had a late dinner at Carrabba's, where they indulged in small talk.

"Kyla tells me you're a flight attendant," Rick said.

It would be just like Ky to pump her up like that to make her seem more glamorous to this guy, but Jessamy was not ashamed of her current choice of profession. East West had been good enough to move her laterally and allowed her to keep her salary at its current level when she needed to slow down to be near her mom. It had been a no-brainer for Jessamy to make the change.

"Former flight attendant. I'm a ticket agent now."

"Isn't that a step back?"

"Depends on one's ambitions."

"Why would you give up traveling the world for a desk job?"

"Personal reasons."

He swirled the wine in his glass. "Which you'd not care to share right now?"

"Exactly." Despite his brazen personal questions, given they'd just met, they had a reasonably good getting-to-know-you first date. Or so she thought.

On the second date, Rick took her to Shula's 347 on Saturday night at the Hotel Duval, and Jessamy was duly impressed. They shared good conversation and the most amazing meal she'd had in a while: Filet mignon, potatoes baked to perfection, a succulent spinach salad, wine she couldn't afford, and key lime pie. It was after dessert that things went south.

"Let's cut to the chase, Jessamy," Rick said. "I find you extremely attractive and Ky says you've been celibate for a while."

Jessamy would kill Ky for over-sharing with her friend/former lover or whatever. The guy was sex on legs, but that's all he was. He didn't even want to pretend that he was after anything more.

"We're both hot enough to ignite some combustible chemistry. What do you say we check into the room I reserved here at the Duval and have some fun?"

Her mood soured upon his blatant proposition. "Is this the new era of dating? Using five-star hotels for booty calls?"

"My housekeeper won't be back until Tuesday, and don't you live with your sick mother? I thought it might be easier if we found a place on neutral ground for our first time."

"You've assumed a whole hell of a lot based on what Kyla told you about me, haven't you, Mr. Traynor?"

"Hell, I was doing her, and by extension you, a favor."

"Thank you very much, Mr. Traynor, but I don't need any favors. In fact, I would appreciate it very much if you'd take me home."

He didn't apologize or respond in any way. He simply signaled for the waiter, paid the check, and escorted Jessamy out of the restaurant. There was an FSU football game, and the guests in attendance were returning to the hotel in droves as they waited for the valet to bring Rick's car around. Jessamy could tell the moment Rick decided he wasn't ready to leave. A trio of blonde, copiously tanned college coeds in cocktail dresses handing out party invitations caught his eye, and the boldest of the three approached him and handed him a flyer.

"The after party of all after parties is at Level 8, starting now," she said, then addressed Jessamy as an afterthought, her eyes blatantly searching out her left hand for a ring. "Bring your girlfriend. It'll be fun."

Rick flashed the blonde a smile that only an unattached interested male would bestow on a woman. "My date's calling it a night, but I might take you up on the invitation."

Jessamy folded her arms, turned her head away from them and rolled her eyes, elaborately. This guy was definitely a piece of work. She made a snap decision and turned to Rick. "Look, I'll take a cab home since you obviously want to go to this party upstairs." Level 8 was the hotel's rooftop club.

Rick reached inside his jacket and pulled out his wallet and thrust two twenties into Jessamy's palm. There was a brief game of push-me pull-you before he finally put the money back and put his wallet away.

His eyes travelled the length of her body. "You sure you don't want to change your mind and join me at Level 8?"

Not if you were the last man on earth.

Jessamy wished she had the nerve to say that to his face and not just in her thoughts. "Thanks, but no thanks," she said instead.

At that he cancelled the call for his car, turned on his heel and followed the blonde trio back into the hotel.

Jessamy approached one of the valet attendants. "Would you mind calling me a cab?"

With a sarcastic laugh, he said, "Good luck with that."

"Tallahassee is not a teeming metropolis. Why can't you call me a cab?"

"Because all the drunk football game patrons are using them right about now. If you wait another hour, I could probably get you one."

"I should've taken that damn forty bucks," she muttered.

"What's that?" the attendant asked.

"Nothing. Thanks. I'll just call a friend to pick me up," she said, as she slid her cell phone out of her purse.

Too angry to call Kyla, Jessamy had to make a choice. A hard choice. One that made the expensive dinner roil in her stomach. Not because she felt bad about calling Griffin. Well, maybe that, too. But calling Griffin meant he was someone she could count on—someone who, regardless of their intimate past, which he'd love to see revived—she could count on him to be there when she needed him.

When she got him on the phone, he didn't ask any questions. He just left their cozy neighborhood and headed downtown immediately to pick her up. Admittedly, this was a role her father might have had were he still alive. It felt practically *middle school* to have an ex rescue her from a date with an asshole, but she was afraid that in her current mood she would say some things to Ky that would sever their decades-long friendship forever.

Even though it was October, the weather still averaged in the high seventies, low eighties and Jessamy had become a drooping mess waiting outside for Griffin. When he pulled up to the curb, his eyes grew wide, and he got out of the car and came around to her.

He grasped her biceps gently and peered into her eyes. "Jess, are you okay?"

"Nothing that a shower and a bottle of merlot can't fix," she said.

She pulled away and went around to the passenger side of Griffin's immaculate BMW, him dogging her steps. She should've known he wouldn't allow her to open the door. Jessamy remembered the story he'd told her about his father teaching him how to treat a lady when he got ready to go to his high school prom. Prior to that, Griffin had never even been on a date.

His long legs overtook her halfway round and he held the door, a grim smile, if there were any such thing, on his handsome face.

"Thank you," she murmured and slid onto the leather seat. Griffin's car somehow managed to keep that new smell despite having had this particular vehicle for at least four years.

Jessamy pulled the visor down and eyed the damage done by the humidity. Hair couldn't be helped, and she wasn't going to bother with refreshing her makeup. The A/C was wicking the excess moisture from her skin, and besides, she didn't have to go to such lengths for Griffin. He wasn't a fan of makeup anyway.

Once they got out of the snarl of post-game revelry traffic, Griffin turned to Jessamy and asked, "So, why didn't this guy bring you home?"

"Oh, he found an after-game party at Level 8 more to his liking."

"Tell me you're not going to go out with this guy again, Jess," Griffin said, a pained look on his face. "You deserve so much more than being abandoned by a Saturday night date."

"I shot myself in the foot, truth be told. He was willing to bring me home; I just didn't want to be in his presence anymore."

"That bad, huh?"

"If you like someone who's a self-aggrandizing asshole masquerading as a straight shooter, I guess it wasn't so bad."

Knowing Griffin as well as she did, she knew he didn't do vague sarcastic answers. A follow-up question was a given.

"What exactly did this moron say, Jessamy?" Then he got downright indignant. "Do I need to turn this car around and kick his ass for offending you? I'm willing to be your Viper to his Mountain, without the cocky attitude."

That Game of Thrones reference endeared him to her in spite of herself. "You'd really defend my honor like a champion of Westeros in the twenty-first century?" Jessamy said, clutching imaginary pearls.

Griffin answered by swerving the car into the left lane in preparation for making a U-turn.

"Griffin, don't you dare turn this car around," she said. Although she really liked this new Griffin. A sort of Clark Kent alpha male who was willing to come to blows with a guy who'd made a pass at her. She wondered if he had an "s" under that Nikola Tesla tee-shirt. The Griffin she'd dated before had been docile and sweet. Less prone to confrontation.

He put his signal on and slowed anyway, as if to turn, and Jessamy yelled. "All right, if I tell you what he said, promise me you won't go back to Hotel Duval?"

"I promise," Griffin said. He flipped off the turn signal and accelerated back onto the thruway.

"He propositioned me after dinner. In fact, he wanted me to accompany him to a room he apparently had waiting for us at the Duval. It was such a forgone-conclusion-after-a-prom-date. So juvenile. I declined and decided he could join the party at Level 8 and try to find someone to replace me. Truth is, he made it abundantly clear he wasn't after anything else."

"His loss," Griffin said.

They rode in silence for a few more seconds before Griffin seemed to light up. "I have a couple of bottles of that merlot you like that we got in St. Augustine that one time. Would you like to share it with me tonight?"

A nightcap between friends. Jessamy could think of nothing she'd like better at the moment. "I'd be delighted."

There was something different about Griffin. An undercurrent of confidence bordering on a swagger he had not possessed before. Jessamy could feel her body responding to this handsome, virile version of the man she had known so intimately before. She squeezed her thighs together and thought of the commanding heights they achieved when he made love to her, only to descend into agonizing depths once the deed was done, and then she relaxed her thighs.

When they arrived at his home, he took her hand and pulled her into the kitchen where he held a seat out for her at the gigantic island at its center, then opened the door to the pantry he'd turned half into a wine rack and retrieved the two bottles in question.

"You know, I feel bad enough after that failed date to drink both of those bottles myself," she said.

Griffin hesitated as he set one and then the other on the bar in front of her. "I could bring out more of a different vintage," he said.

"Just kidding," she said with a grin. "If I drank both, you'd probably end up holding my hair at the end of the evening, and that's not a good look on me."

His mouth quirked up on one side as he reached into the cabinets and brought out pristine stemware. When he carried everything to his sitting room, they got comfortable on the sofa; soft music played in the background, and Griffin poured them both a generous glass and proposed a toast.

"To old friends starting over as new friends," he said and touched his glass to hers.

Clearly, Griffin wanted another chance with her, but she wasn't sure if she could withstand what them being together again would entail.

Jessamy proposed a lighter, less intimate toast. "To creepy dates. May neither of us have any of those ever again!"

"Hear, hear," Griffin said, and they drank almost in perfect synchronicity.

"So these are really the last two bottles of that case you bought?" Jessamy took another sip, the smoky, natural sweetness bursting on her tongue.

"Yes. I gave a few bottles away as gifts, because I really never wanted to drink it with anyone besides you."

She turned away slightly embarrassed by the earnestness in his eyes and in his words. Griffin drew her back into conversation and they caught up on what had happened in each other's lives in the two years after they parted.

They talked a good bit about his work, probably because that was his default comfort setting. He was always surprised that Jessamy knew a good deal about science in general and the type of work he did. She'd been a science major in college before she changed in her junior year because the labs and all the dissections got to be too much. Also, because of her father's cancer she'd learned a fair share about his radiological treatments.

When conversation faltered, Griffin stood and extended a hand to her. "Dance?"

Jessamy stood in answer. She absolutely loved dancing with Griffin. He made her feel like she knew her way around a dance floor. In fact, Griffin reminded Jessamy a bit of the actor Brendan Fraser when he danced, and the character he played in the movie *Blast From the Past*, only without the slow and deliberate speech pattern.

Jessamy laughed, flushed to the point of breathlessness by one of his dance moves. Her stomach churned as she wondered when—not if—he was going to make a real move. When the song came on which she'd heard Griffin whistle on more than one occasion, she gasped.

"You whistle this tune all the time," Jessamy said as she floated in his arms across the dance floor.

"Do you know it?"

"Frank Sinatra, right?"

"Yes, it's *Fly Me To The Moon*. My parents played this music a lot as I was growing up and it wasn't until I was about twelve that I decided to ask them why they liked this particular song so much."

"Why do they like it so much?"

"It was their wedding song," Griffin said. "You know how you hear something so much you eventually begin to sing or hum it? That's why I whistle this tune, and it's done as much in habit as to honor my parents, or when I'm extremely happy about something."

When he dipped her low after the song ended, Jessamy was sure Griffin would kiss her then, but he showed incredible restraint.

Their conversation eventually meandered to their mutual love.

"So, what say you about the last season of *Game of Thrones*?" Jessamy asked with uncharacteristic coyness, especially with Griffin. "Did you watch?"

"Yes. And I loved it," he declared. "Peter Dinklage is amazing as the Imp, isn't he?"

"Yes, he's great," she said. "I told you the first season there was an Emmy in his future."

He nodded in agreement. "I only have you to blame for the dark circles I sport around my eyes during Game of Thrones season," he said, with an endearing smile. "I sometimes watch the episodes over again immediately after they've aired."

Jessamy laughed. "Would you like me to make you a pot of coffee, then?"

"Change that to breakfast in the morning, and only if you'll join me."

Jessamy's heart pounded when she realized he might be picking up on the fact that she might not be opposed to something happening between them. He didn't act on it right away; he just topped off their glasses again.

They grew more and more tipsy as they consumed each glass of wine poured. Then, when the second bottle was emptied shortly after midnight, Jessamy reached over and took Griffin's large hand in her own.

Jessamy felt a wave of attraction and hoped he wanted to kiss her as much as she wanted to kiss him, or at least test the waters to make sure her feelings weren't completely one-sided. Griffin was a great kisser and Jessamy was anxious to see if this were still the case, but Griffin, as per usual, insisted on taking things slow to the point of crawling. He merely laced his fingers with hers. This was frustrating for Jessamy, because for two people who were germophobic and squeamish, they certainly didn't have a lot of trouble with exploring basic chemistry before.

To her utter delight he finally picked up on her blatant invitation and gave her a brief, nervous kiss on the lips. She remembered his lips were softer and fuller than average, and though he broke the kiss far sooner than she would've liked, there was a tinge of heat that hinted of things to come. She wanted to knock over furniture, strip him naked, and climb his torso like a tree. Of course she would tidy everything back up afterward, but he made her want to throw caution to the wind. To luxuriate in the passion she knew they could produce together.

Emboldened by his response, she kissed him again the same way he had kissed her when they'd taken the Poconos trip together, and so many times more after that she couldn't count them. She'd missed his kisses. She'd missed his gentle, yet passionate way of making love to her until she was no longer coherent—as if she were intoxicated with wine—but was just intoxicated with a lot of Griffin. In that moment, she wanted that again and she took it.

Griffin did not resist her advances, and soon they were kissing their way down the hall and into his bed. To his credit, Griffin abbreviated his bedtime ritual to the point of non-existence and they were writhing on his bed within minutes, much to Jessamy's sheer surprise.

Maybe it was the wine, or perhaps the realization that his kindness made her want to be with him again after suffering a humiliating date with someone who didn't care about her, or the idea that they were coming together again for the first time in two years. Truth is, it was most likely the fact that Jessamy, after all this time, was still so in awe of Griffin's physique under his conservative clothing, she was willing to do just about anything to get with him again.

Griffin, who Jessamy was sure had been abstinent for the time they were apart, emerged with a ferocity she'd never witnessed in him before. Foreplay ranged from sweet to intense and yielded two orgasms for her before Griffin finally aligned himself with her and entered her in one swift motion. They both groaned in their joining with the sound of two who had been denied sex for quite some time, then synchronized their rhythm in the manner of longtime lovers almost immediately. Jessamy felt like she was being catapulted out of the stratosphere and perhaps to the moon with Griffin's passionately precise lovemaking.

"Jess!" He said, in a voice graveled with passion. "It's been so long."

She knew exactly what he meant. He wasn't going to last long this first time, but that was okay. He had taken care of her so thoroughly beforehand she didn't mind that he would finish before her this time.

When the spasms signifying his release came, Jessamy wound her legs tightly around his spectacular ass and rode his climax out with him. It felt so good to have a man again, she gloried in holding and being held by him. Then they slept, the complete and exhausted sleep of sated lovers.

≪ Chapter 5 ≫

Jessamy awoke with a start, hyper-aware that she wasn't in her own bedroom. It immediately dawned on her that she was in Griffin's bed, his warm body curled around her. His front to her back. Morning wood wedged between her legs as if it belonged there. He loved to spoon almost as much as hugging her from behind when they were vertical.

Courtesy of his ever-present breathing strip taped across his nose, Griffin didn't snore, so there wasn't a cue to let her know he was awake. She felt Griffin stir behind her instead. "You awake, Jess?"

"Yes."

"Are you regretting what happened between us?"

Way to cut to the chase, Dr. Sanderson.

Jessamy turned to face him with a smile. "No. Are you?"

He grinned, an action that took several years off his already youthful looking thirty-six. "Absolutely not."

Jessamy brushed his lips slightly with hers, knowing that neither of them would welcome a deeper kiss before some serious tooth-brushing happened. She was about to roll away, but Griffin surprised her by pulling her closer. Whatever he was undergoing to counteract his OCD seemed to be working wonders.

"I didn't mean to ply you with alcohol and take advantage of you," he said with a smile. "But now that I have you here, let's see if an encore will give us even better results."

Jessamy eagerly obliged him.

"Look what the cat dragged in," Clarice said when Jessamy unlocked the kitchen door and walked into her home.

"Morning, Mama," she said and went to the pot to pour herself yet another cup of coffee. She'd had breakfast with Griffin, complete with coffee, but wasn't sure the new Griffin was changed enough not to comment on her propensity to drink all the coffee until it was gone.

Clarice was doing breakfast dishes. "You want something to eat, baby?"

"No, I've had breakfast." She sat at the bar and watched Clarice wash, rinse, then stack the dishes in the dishwasher. Jessamy pondered whether she should allow her mother to believe she'd slept with Rick on the second date, or correct that and tell her that she'd slept with Griffin after a couple of years hiatus from their former love affair. Talk about a rock and a hard place.

Clarice finished up and dried her hands after she put the last dish away. "Whew!" Clarice huffed and sat next her daughter. "You're a little too old to be doing the walk of shame, aren't you?"

Jessamy grinned. "What do you know about the walk of shame, old lady?"

"That type of thing happened in my day, too. They didn't just make that up for the younger set, I'll have you know."

Jessamy sipped her coffee and gathered her courage. "I spent the night at Griffin's, Mama."

Clarice looked at her over her glasses. "Say what?"

Jessamy knew her mother's response was rhetorical; better yet, she was shocked at the recent turn of events.

"You left with that Rick Train . . . "

"Traynor," she corrected.

"Whatever," Clarice said. "How did this happen?"

"Well, when a man and woman are attracted to each other . . ."

Her mother rolled her eyes. "Don't get all sarcastic with me, baby girl."

"I'll be thirty in two months, Mama. But, I'll take being called a girl over an old maid any day."

"You know people don't even keep to those old customs anymore. Young women are waiting longer and longer to be married."

"I know, but they're not necessarily forgoing companionship. I can't seem to keep a man."

"You and Griffin getting back together?"

Jessamy sighed. "I don't know."

"He's not the type to toy with a woman's heart, Jess. Not Griffin."

Jessamy knew her mother had always liked Griffin better than any boyfriend she'd ever had. Even her father, before he passed, had seemed disappointed when things hadn't worked out for Jessamy and Griffin the first time.

Her mother adjusted her oxygen tank and stood. "Maybe next time you see him, you two should spend more time talking than on . . . other activities," Clarice said and sashayed out of the room.

Jessamy's face grew warm. Having her mother know that she'd had sex never got any better. No matter how old she was.

Griffin used an invitation to the Tallahassee Saturday Morning Marketplace Downtown as his opportunity to discuss the same topic he'd sought Jessamy out to discuss just before her ill-fated date with Rick Traynor. Her attempt to invite her mother along as a buffer didn't work.

"You two go on," Clarice said. "It'll be too warm out for me in short order."

As they were backing out of her driveway in Griffin's car he ribbed her good-naturedly. "So, it's come to that, has it?"

"To what?" Jessamy asked, continuing her pretense of not knowing.

"Bringing your mother along on a date so you won't have to talk to me."

"Pfftt!" Jessamy made a noncommittal noise but she knew he was right. "Besides, what would we have to talk about that my mother couldn't be around to hear?"

"What happened last night for starters."

Jessamy folded her arms. "We were two lonely, vulnerable people with an intimate past who succumbed to passion after a night of generous imbibing."

"So, you're going to go with that, are you?"

"What else is there, Griffin?"

"You left out the part about us caring for one another."

Jessamy looked hopeful. "We do?"

"I would think so," he said. "You know, Jess, our problem never was about not caring, it was always about my disorder, and how it sabotaged our relationship before we could get to the next level."

Deep down, she knew this, but did not want to assume their hook-up had been anything more unless that was his intention, and it seemed like that was his intention.

"So, you'd like us to resume where we left off a couple of years ago?"

"That would be an emphatic yes," he said with a grin, then sobered. "I've missed you, Jess."

She was so overcome with emotion, she could barely speak above a whisper, "I've missed you, too Griffin." It was the truth. Despite the way his issues affected their relationship, she missed how kind and attentive he was. How he entered her world when he really didn't have to. How he spoiled her to the point that no other man ever measured up.

He reached across the console and took her hand, and drove happily one-handed to their destination.

Griffin found a parking space just as the Mercat March began. A blast of bagpipe music rang through the streets to signify the opening of the Marketplace. The Downtown Marketplace began its normal buzzing of activity as it does each and every Saturday it's open from March to November. Located in Ponce de Leon and Bloxham Parks along Park

Avenue and Monroe Streets, the Marketplace is *the* Saturday morning destination for a lot of locals.

Griffin actually held her hand as they strolled in the park checking out the vendors' wares, without fidgeting. Without his palm sweating, without making an excuse to do so as he might have before. Because spontaneity used to scare the hell out of him. Now he embraced it.

After they'd made the rounds through the various booths, stopping to see things up close that caught their interest and making a couple of purchases, they walked, again hand-in-hand, back to Griffin's car to stow them.

Once their purchases were secure in the trunk, Griffin gestured back toward the Marketplace. "So, would you like to have lunch here, or find a place where we can sit and talk?"

Jessamy was flummoxed by that offer. "You'd really eat here?" The Griffin she'd known before never ate food from open-air vendors. Too many opportunities for germs, insects, and/or miniscule dust particles to land on his food.

"Why not?" he said, cocking his head to the side in that adorable way he had of doing. "But it's your choice."

Whereas before, he would cock his head just so and it would be quite a few moments before he replied, Jessamy no longer had to wait for him to over-think before speaking. Now he spoke decisively, and it did not rob him of that air of authority the other way had given him. He was still brilliant Griffin, just without the abundance of strange hang-ups. There were just a stark few, now.

"I'm flexible," he declared.

They feasted on gigantic turkey legs, sweet corn on the cob, funnel cake, and fresh lemonade as they lounged on a park bench. Jessamy shared her hand sanitizer wipes with him before and after the meal, since he had, oddly, not come prepared. This was so unlike him, she had to ask about it once he'd discarded the trash in a nearby receptacle.

"I know you started seeing a therapist after we parted ways before," she said. "If this is the result, it's quite an achievement."

Griffin's lips quirked into a half smile, and he took her hand in his, threading their fingers together. "I was determined to get better so I could be in a relationship with a woman without embarrassing myself all the time. I particularly wanted you to see that I could change. That I could be normal enough for you."

"For me?"

"Yes. For you."

"Normal enough?"

He chuckled. "Let's face it Jess, you use so much hand sanitizer you should purchase stock in it."

Griffin had jokes. She teased back, "Well, you wash your hands more than I sanitize mine."

"I have to wash my hands often. It's required of us healthcare professionals."

"Then, you need to invest in hand lotion." She squeezed his hand for effect.

"This from the woman who showers immediately before and after sex."

"So do you!"

"Only because it makes you happy. I could settle for just going after."

"No you couldn't. The dry heaves might turn into puking again if I weren't squeaky clean before you touched me."

"That has nothing to do with my perception of your cleanliness. It has to do with the fact that as a scientist I know what resides on our bodies, even when we've taken every step possible to get ourselves clean."

"I think maybe a bit of hypnosis might be in order, then."

"Why?"

"Because if this is going to work between us, I can't have you going all Billy Bob Thornton on me when we make love."

"Please stop comparing me to that *Monster's Ball* character."

"If you'll stop insisting I'm as abnormal as you are."

He leaned in and kissed her lips. This PDA was new, too. "We're both as mad as hatters. That's why it works between us."

"You just keep thinking that, Dr. Sanderson."

"So," he said, as he stood and pulled her up to join him. "Are we agreed that we're going to try this again?"

Her heart stuttered in her chest, the look in his eyes was so rapacious.

"Yes," she said, and fell into step with him as they sauntered toward his car.

Jessamy liked this new Griffin, so much so, she wanted to put a sign on her forehead that said, "Keep Calm, and like this new Griffin."

≪ Chapter 6 ≫

"This chicken is delicious, Ky," Jessamy said.

Kyla made her dinner as a peace offering for sending her on that disastrous date, and on a week night, no less. They'd been friends long enough to not let petty grievances keep them apart for long. The conversation about Rick Traynor done, they were enjoying one another's company again.

"Thanks, Jess. Glad you like it."

"You've got to tell me how you prepared this. I want to cook it for Griffin and me."

Smirking, Kyla narrowed her eyes at her over the table. "So, you really are giving it another go with Mr. Germophobia, huh?"

"Don't call him that. It's not like he can help being the way he is. At least now he's working on changing."

Kyla nibbled on an asparagus spear. "Touchy, touchy. I'm okay with it, as long as he doesn't make me wash my hands before he'll shake mine again, we're cool."

"I don't think he'll do that," Jessamy said, not altogether sure he would extend the same courtesy to others as he was extending to her now.

"Okay, just don't come whining to me if he has a relapse," Kyla said. "So, what caused the change anyway?"

"Well, he started seeing a therapist shortly after we broke up, which I encouraged him to do. Dr. Upton had helped me a lot with my issues, and I thought he could really help Griffin."

"Why is it that men, regardless of their professions, are so resistant to medical help?"

"I know, right? I remember my dad being like that. Is Carter also that way?"

"Yes! I had to threaten to dump him before he agreed to get a routine physical. He hadn't had one in three years. Can you believe that?"

"Griffin isn't like that with his physical health. I think on some level he believed his OCD was logical given his scientific training, I mean vomiting after sex not-withstanding."

"So, no chunk-blowing this time around?"

"Nary a chunk was blown all weekend," Jessamy said.

"This is good," Kyla said. "Now you can concentrate on really getting your freak on with him, rather than avoiding sex like you two did before."

"Thanks, Dr. Phil," Jessamy teased. "And, let's change the subject, because I'm not liking this as a dinner conversation."

"Oh, come on now, what's a bit of Ralph humor between friends with strong constitutions?" Kyla said, and held her wine glass out, which Jessamy promptly clinked.

For Jessamy, dating Griffin this time around was more enjoyable than surreal. No longer was he a cross between *The Big Bang Theory's* main characters. Now it was like dating *A Beautiful Mind*, a John Nash with no mental health issues, who had the social graces and the physical goods to back it up. They fell into a similar routine as before, making his schedule work with hers so they could spend quality time together when he was in town.

Before, Jessamy had believed Griffin treated her so well because he was over-compensating for his disorder. She soon found out that his *modus operandi* had not changed much. He still brought insignificant little gifts when he came to dinner at her home, this time for her and her mother. He was also probably one of the most unselfish lovers ever, because he made sure her needs were met to the detriment of his own sometimes. Jessamy found herself falling for him again very quickly, even though she didn't believe they'd ever gotten to the point of actually being in love before.

They began to watch their favorite television shows together again, especially during their Tuesday or Wednesday night dinners, depending on which schedule week he was in. This time, they were able to watch *The Big Bang Theory* together without him feeling uncomfortable. In fact there was a fair amount of self-deprecation when he recognized some of his vagaries in Leonard and Sheldon.

Griffin was originally a TV snob, and more a nerdy fan boy of classic comics, graphic novels books and medical journals. Besides the odd news, science or sports show, he was decidedly not well-versed on the finer points of popular culture. Jessamy found this oddly adorable about him.

As the holidays began to approach, around Thanksgiving, a colleague gave Griffin tickets to an FSU football game. Usually he declined such offers because of the crowds bearing untold germs of the bacterial, viral, and fungal varieties. He wasn't overly concerned about those of the protozoal variety unless he were going barefoot or ingesting impure water, so his usual reasons not to go to places where large crowds congregated had to do with airborne germs.

"Are you sure you want to get up close and personal with eighty thousand people at Doak Campbell Stadium?" Jessamy asked.

"We've been to the Marketplace, to the Flea Market, and to concerts at the Civic Center recently," he said. "I think I'm ready to try Doak, especially if we're going to spend Christmas in New York City."

They had made tentative plans for a destination holiday this year, much like their trip to the Poconos the first year they'd dated, but this time, Griffin wanted to swing by his parents' home in Ithaca, introduce her mother and reintroduce Jessamy and spend a couple of days with them. Jessamy was concerned that her mother wouldn't be comfortable being foisted upon his parents while they ventured into the city, but Clarice had other ideas. Her favorite cousin lived in White Plains, so she would spend the few days Griffin and Jessamy would be in the city with her cousin. Problem solved.

When game day came, they dressed comfortably in FSU jerseys and blue jeans, wearing shades to shield the sun from their eyes, and generous amounts of sunscreen coating their exposed skin. They even tailgated with a group from the hospital, and Griffin's participation for the first time was the topic of conversation for the first ten minutes or so. Then everyone relaxed and began to have fun.

"Hey Jessamy," the wife of one of the radiologists said. "It's so good to finally meet you. We were beginning to think you were Griffin's imaginary friend since he never brought you to any of our shindigs before."

It was true, she'd never entered his work world, despite the many times he'd entered hers. She didn't think it was some deliberate slight on his part, just fear that his awkward social malaise would overshadow any function they might be invited to attend. Jessamy was excited to finally be included in this part of Griffin's life.

"Now you know. Griffin is not Lars, and I'm a real girl," Jessamy joked.

The woman bumped her beer bottle to Jessamy's and laughed. "Griffin looks better than Ryan Gosling anyway."

And these days he's a lot less creepy. Jessamy felt slightly guilty for thinking that, but it was true. Whatever Griffin was doing to lessen the effect of his OCD was working very well. She guessed it was some combination of behavior therapy and medication, because that's what it had taken for her all those years ago.

Jessamy mentally shook herself and sought Griffin out where he was huddled with a group of couples near the grill. He pulled her into the circle of his arms, his front to her back, resting his head atop hers as he listened to his colleagues holding court.

"Having fun?" he murmured.

"Yes! Thanks for rescuing me from Black Friday shopping with my mother," she said.

"My pleasure," Griffin said, and squeezed her close.

They'd spent the night at his place the night before since her mother said she had some mysterious *plans.* Jessamy didn't question her. She just assumed Clarice was staying with the friend she was going shopping with.

An hour later, they were in the stadium cheering on the Seminoles against their arch rivals, the Florida Gators. Once upon a time neither of them would've been able to handle such a large crowd of people without having a panic attack, but they were actually watching a live football game, and cheering right along with some eighty odd thousand of their closest friends.

≪ Chapter 7 ≫

"Hey, Jess. I'll be running a bit late for dinner. Will you walk down to my house and take the steaks out of the freezer when you get home? See you around seven-thirty." She was more than halfway home when she played her voice messages hands-free so she didn't have to be distracted by the traffic.

Jessamy listened to the message on her cellphone twice, simply because she liked hearing Griffin's voice. As she turned into their neighborhood, she wondered what emergency had kept Griffin occupied at the hospital after hours. She pulled into her garage and entered her kitchen to greet her mother and change before she headed over to Griffin's.

She rejoined her mother in the kitchen, pulling her hair back into a ponytail. She would use Griffin's exercise equipment while she was unthawing the steaks, then come back home for a shower before they met for dinner at seven-thirty. Clarice had also changed, she noticed.

"Hey, Mama. Are you going to Bingo tonight?"

"That's the plan," Clarice said.

Jessamy grabbed a bottle of water out of the fridge. "I'm having dinner with Griffin, so I'll make sure we grill a steak for you for later, if you want."

Clarice was fidgeting with her outfit and Jessamy noticed her mother was wearing a bit more makeup than her customary lipstick only.

"That's all right, baby. I'm going out to dinner with a friend after Bingo."

"Male or female?" Jessamy said with a smirk.

Her mother huffed. "Why would you ask that?"

"Because you're all spiffed up," she said. "What gives, Mom?"

Clarice stood up straight. "I'm having dinner with a nice, retired FAMU college professor I've been friends with at Bingo for quite some time. He's the first man there I've felt was worthy of my time."

"I think it's good you've met someone," Jessamy said. "Daddy would want you to have companionship." Although her father had been a Tuskegee graduate and she wasn't sure what he would think of his wife dating a Florida A&M professor, one of their biggest rivals.

Clarice's eyes shimmered with unshed tears. "Are you okay with it though? Truly?"

Jessamy held her arms out and closed the distance between them, wrapping her diminutive mother in her arms. She cleared her throat of the lump that had taken residence there. "Absolutely!"

"I'll introduce you to him when he drops me off tonight," her mother said, beaming. Jessamy couldn't remember the last time she had seen her mother so happy since her father's death.

Retrieving Griffin's spare key from his combination-locked hiding place just beneath an antique bird feeder, Jessamy let herself in. It was after five, so thankfully the air conditioning, which was set to lower itself right before Griffin came home each day, was already on. Jessamy had done this, too, before her mother moved in, so she couldn't blame him for conserving energy in this way.

Everything was as immaculately tidy as it always was, and Jessamy went straight to the pricey sub-zero refrigerator freezer combo he'd had installed when he first bought the house and pulled out the rib eyes. She set them in the sink and ran cold water over them to thaw naturally in their vacuum sealed packaging.

Griffin would cut them open just before he was ready to season them and put them on the grill. Old habits died hard, and she was sure he wanted the meat to spend as little time in the open air as possible. That quirk she could handle.

She squeezed a liberal amount of hand soap from the dispenser next to his dishwashing detergent and washed her hands thoroughly in the other sink. Then, throwing her towel across her shoulder she went down the hall to his exercise room. She first did a half hour on the elliptical, and then switched to the treadmill for a sprint and then a short walk to cool down.

Taking a gander at her watch, she saw she'd timed it perfectly. She decided if the steaks were almost thawed, she would open them, put them in a container to marinate and leave around six-thirty and that would give her plenty of time to go home, shower and dress for their casual dinner.

She quickly seasoned the steaks in a small Pyrex dish, put the lid on it, and set them in the fridge. As she was washing her hands again, Griffin's answering machine came on. Yeah, he was even old-school with some of his gadgets. Most people used the telephone company's answering service, but not Griffin.

"Hey Griffin, Tate here."

Oh, it was Dr. Upton, her very own psychiatrist. Of course he and Griffin would be on a first name basis because they were colleagues at the hospital.

"I know you're busy, but you need to get back in to see me. If everything went well and you were able to convince your ex to help with your Exposure and Response Prevention Therapy, we can begin to taper you off the medication over several months and see if just the Cognitive Behavior Therapy and ERP combined are as effective alone as they were with the medication. Call me, buddy."

All the blood drained from Jessamy's face. Is that all she'd been to Griffin over the past several weeks? A guinea pig? She stalked out of his house and slammed the door. She didn't realize she'd left his spare key on the counter in his kitchen until she was re-entering her own house, but she didn't care much about that at the moment. She went straight to her bedroom, stripped out of her sweaty clothes, and hopped into the shower. The difference in temperature of the water and the tears streaming down her face was the only thing that clued her in that she was crying until her body quaked and the sound of sobbing joined the hot tears.

Jessamy's cell phone vibrated again for the umpteenth time and she ignored it. Again. She paced her best friend's bedroom floor while Kyla put the finishing touches on her makeup.

"You know he's just going to keep calling until he gets you, right," Kyla said. "That OCD is still in there somewhere and he's not going to let this go."

"I don't give a flying fuck," Jessamy said. Her chest burned as if someone had reached into it and pulled her heart out.

Kyla flinched. Jessamy wasn't normally the one who threw around f-bombs. "Whoa, girlfriend. So, are you going to tell me what he did to piss you off so badly before I leave to meet Carter at his boss's dinner party?"

"Apparently, Griffin was supposed to use me to make sure his therapy was working. And stupid me, I thought he decided to get better because he wanted to be back with me."

"Well, look at it this way, he chose you rather than some random skank at a night club." Kyla stood up from her vanity. "I know it's rather off-putting to think you were just a means to an end for him or something, but from what you've told me, that's not how he's been treating you."

"No, but I would've liked to have known I was being used."

"Back up just a minute, Jess. How did you find this out, anyway? Did Griffin suddenly get a guilty conscience and called you up and told you this?"

"No." Jessamy wrung her hands. "Actually, I overheard Dr. Upton on his answering machine while I was at his house unthawing steak."

"Wait a minute. Tell me exactly what Dr. Upton said." Jessamy recited his message as closely to the original as she could remember.

"He said, 'If you were able to convince your ex to help with your Exposure and Response Prevention Therapy, we can begin to taper you off the medication.' I'm the only ex Griffin's had, so he had to be talking about me."

"Aw, Jess," Kyla said, and pulled her in for a hug. She held Jessamy at arm's length and looked into her eyes. "Think about this, though. Would you have rather he tried such an intimate thing with someone else, before coming back to you?"

"Who's to say he ever intended to come back to me except to give his new treatment a test run. Maybe I was so sad and needy Griffin just felt sorry for me."

"Look, I've got to go, but feel free to stay here as long as you like, but if I were you, I'd go talk to Griffin. I'm sure he has an explanation for this. You just have to be open enough to listen."

"I'll think about it," Jessamy said. She feigned as well as she could that she was okay until Kyla was out the door, then the waterworks began anew.

Jessamy remembered just before nine that her mother promised to introduce her to her new friend. She hopped into her car and raced back to the cul-de-sac. She pulled into her driveway next to a late model Chevy Impala which had to belong to her mother's friend. She hoped she hadn't kept them too long.

Griffin had to have been lying in wait for her, because she had barely turned off the ignition and was grabbing her purse when he came barreling down the sidewalk. He snatched her car door open and pulled her into his arms.

"Jessamy, I've been worried sick," he said, his voice thick and husky with emotion. "Where have you been? I saw the steaks in the fridge and my spare key on the counter, so I knew you'd come by, but then radio silence."

Jessamy pushed him away and stepped back. "When were you going to tell me I was your unwitting partner for your ERP Therapy, Griffin?"

He rubbed a hand across his face and into his hair, a move that made thick, inky strands stand up every which way, and would've been funny if she weren't so angry.

"I was going to tell you, but then you had that crappy date at the Duval, and you were so down about that. Then we drank wine and ended up in bed together, and I just didn't want to say, 'Guess what, Jess? You just proved my therapy is working.'"

"But that's what your urgency was to get back to me, wasn't it?"

"It was the intention at first, but believe me when I say, Jess, the last few weeks have been better than I've ever imagined things could be between us. I did all of it because of you."

At that moment, her mother peeked her head out the front door. "I thought I heard a car pull up out here. Bring Griffin in with you so he can meet John," her mother said.

"Griffin has to go, Mama," she yelled back, keeping her eyes trained on his. Then she lowered her voice. "I need some time to think, Griffin. Will you at least give me that?"

"While you're thinking," he said, his anger now palpable, "remember I never wanted us to break up. As fucked up as our situation was before, I still wanted you, even when you didn't want me."

He turned and walked back to his home and didn't look back once.

≪ Chapter 8 ≫

It only took her mother a few weeks to figure out that something was amiss with Jessamy and Griffin. Clarice likely would've figured it out earlier if she hadn't been so smitten with Professor John Carlton, III. When she returned from Bingo one Wednesday night, Clarice found Jessamy in her room lying listlessly on her bed watching reruns of *The Big Bang Theory*, a half-eaten bowl of Orville Redenbacher microwaved popcorn sitting on the bed next to her.

"Don't you and Griffin have standing dinner plans on Wednesday nights?"

"When he's in town," Jessamy said.

Her mother moved to her dresser, looking at perfume bottle labels. "Then he's out of town?"

"I don't know." Jessamy muted the television.

"Thank you. I don't see what folks see in that show, anyway," Clarice said. "All that talk about science and those weird characters."

"That's just it, they're all smart. They're nerds. Except this one girl in the building."

"Kind of like you and Griffin, then," Clarice said. "I get it. It's usually opposites that attract for whatever reason. I know you think that because you and Griffin have this OCD thing in common, you're too much alike to really get along. Well, that's what you thought before."

"Griffin was resistant to getting help before, Mama. That's why we broke up the last time."

"What about this time?"

Jessamy really looked at her mother then. "How'd you know?"

"He hasn't been around here, and you haven't been slipping over to his place in the middle of the night like you'd been doing."

"I thought I was careful to get home before you woke up in the morning."

"Girl, please. Even when you slipped out in high school, I knew it."

"And I thought Kyla and I had pulled one over on you and Dad."

"Baby, you've got to get up early in the morning to fool me," Clarice said. "I remember loving the Jackson Five so much, I slipped out to go to their concert once. You deserved that same experience with a band you loved."

"I'm glad you and Dad didn't bust us and ground me."

"I said *I* knew. I didn't say anything about your Daddy knowing."

Jessamy's eyes widened. "Oh."

Clarice sniffed one of the bottles she'd been checking out on the dresser. "So, what's up with you and Griffin?"

Jessamy sat all the way up and swung her feet onto the floor. "What if you found out that Professor Carlton started going out with you for a reason other than just wanting to get to know you better?"

"Is that what you think Griffin did?"

"That's what I know Griffin did. This time."

Clarice went and sat next to her daughter and gazed into her eyes. "Listen, Jessamy, my one and only daughter. That awkward man has been in love with you from the get go. Now, I don't know why he couldn't be upfront about why he came back into your life this time, but you can take it to the bank. That man loves you."

"I thought he was just treating me so nice because that's how his father taught him to treat a lady."

"That may be true, but he went the extra mile with you, baby."

"I know he was always kind to me and treated me with respect, but his quirks drove me crazy."

"Maybe they drove you crazy because you were resisting falling in love with him."

"Now that sounds crazy."

"I promised Griffin I wouldn't say anything, especially while your father was alive, but you need to know what kind of man you're trying to throw away a second time."

Jessamy looked into her mother's eyes. "Your father didn't just change doctors to make it easy for you to date Griffin," Clarice said. "I encouraged him to change because I knew that Griffin was going to pay for that procedure your father got that prolonged his life beyond what the chemo and radiation was doing for him."

"But I thought Daddy had great insurance from his old job with Case Engineering."

"That he did, but some treatments aren't covered by insurance."

"Why would Griffin do that for Daddy?"

"No man would do that for a woman's father unless he truly loved that woman."

"Really?"

"Really. And usually, everybody else can see it except you, too. But a little forgiveness can go a long way in reconciling your differences."

"I've been so stupid. I should never have doubted how Griffin felt about me, this time or the last. Why didn't he tell me how he felt?"

"Because when he was getting ready to, you were too busy breaking up with him. Men are prideful, baby, and we have to let them keep that sometimes. He wanted to prove to you that he could change before he pursued you again, so he went to see Dr. Upton so he could be a better man for you."

"I was afraid to love him when I knew his issues were tearing us apart, but if I'd known about what he did for Daddy back then, I wouldn't have been able to leave him. Just like I shouldn't have been thinking about leaving him this time."

"What you waiting on, then? I think you might owe each other apologies, or something. No time like the present to settle things. You two have let too many suns go down on your anger."

Jessamy hugged her mother close. "Thanks, Mama."

She called Griffin, first on his home phone. No answer. She walked down to his house and peeked through the window of his garage. His car wasn't there.

Then she tried him on his cell.

He must be in Miami.

Since their falling out, he had not taken his regular flights when she was on duty. He'd completely changed his schedule and avoided her completely. She really couldn't blame him. She'd refused to give him the benefit of the doubt when he needed it most. He'd had so much rejection as a young man. That was probably all he ever expected from the opposite sex, even as an adult.

Jessamy was working on her birthday, and Christmas was a week away. It seemed she was doomed to spend another special occasion and another holiday alone. Well, at least she had work. She was busy checking in an unusually full, actually over-booked flight to Miami concurrently with a full flight to Tampa. The line was so long it snaked from her counter and zig-zagged like a maze so intricately, she couldn't see the end of it. Thankfully, there were still two hours before the flight would board, and she and her team worked with an inhuman precision trying to ensure everyone got through in time to board their flights.

The whistling of "Fly Me to the Moon" made the fine hairs on the back of her neck stand to attention. Griffin was in line. After weeks of avoiding her, driving straight into his garage when he was working at home, and varying his trash schedule from hers, checking in online and checking his luggage curbside, he was actually now physically in her line. The idea that she would see him shortly made her work the line faster, and her frenzy made her co-workers ramp up, too.

Finally, she could see him. He was the last person in line, and if someone came behind him, he would graciously allow them to go ahead of him. What was his deal? Talk about mixed signals. Did he want to see her, or not? She'd missed him so much she was ready to abandon her counter, climb his exceptionally toned body and kiss him until their PDA made everyone in the terminal sick of them.

Did she dare make the first move? His being there was actually the first move, so he deserved to have her make some grand gesture. When there were five people left to serve before Griffin, Jessamy turned to her co-worker, Susan.

"Will you take over from here? I'm going to take a break."

"Sure thing," Susan said, and then whispered. "Good timing. Don't look now, but WG is in the line."

"You mean, Dr. Sanderson, right?" she said in a no nonsense tone. Susan's eyes bulged like a cartoon character's. Jessamy didn't often pull rank, but she was tired of her co-workers making fun of the man she loved.

She walked round the counter and made a beeline for Griffin who stood tall and proud in line behind four other people now waiting for his turn at the ticket counter. His eyes followed her, his head cocked to one side, his brow knit in curiosity.

Jessamy walked right up to him, grabbed his tie and pulled his lips down to hers. Griffin only briefly hesitated then kissed her back just as intensely as she was kissing him. The people left in the line cheered and made catcalls, and when they came up for air, Jessamy saw the stunned looks on her co-workers faces.

As they waited for the last few people to be processed through, Jessamy linked her arm through Griffin's and looked up into his eyes. "I'm sorry," she said simply.

"I'm sorry, too," he said. "I should've told you what Dr. Upton wanted me to do. I shouldn't have allowed you to seduce me while you were in such a vulnerable state."

She grinned. "I seduced you?"

"Isn't that what happened since you kissed me first that night?" His affected air of innocence was priceless.

Jessamy laughed. "That is exactly what happened, and I shouldn't have freaked out just because I learned you were doing exactly what your doctor asked you to do. I should have been honored to help you with your therapy. By the way, if that's an ongoing therapy you need to participate in, you can count me in from here on out."

"It is ongoing. However, I'm on my way to Miami, and I had this insane idea that I would kidnap my ticket agent and take her with me for her birthday." He reached into his briefcase and handed her an elaborately wrapped gift and a card.

Jessamy's jaw dropped. "You remembered."

"How could I forget?"

She tiptoed and gave him another peck on the lips as thanks. "You actually want me to go to work with you?"

"Well, not to work with me, but when I'm not working, we can practice a little therapy together in my hotel suite."

"I would love to do that, but my mother—"

"Is spending the rest of the week at Professor Carlton's place."

"They make such a cute couple, don't they?"

"Yes, and I can't believe I've just agreed to calling a couple 'cute.' So, my plans for kidnapping you are a go. Right, Ms. Taylor?"

"Yes, Dr. Sanderson. Your plans are a go."

The final customer taken care of, Susan greeted them. "Dr. Sanderson, Ms. Taylor. I actually have your tickets here," she said with a smile. Then she reached behind the counter and handed Jessamy her purse and an overnight bag.

"You knew he had a ticket for me all along, didn't you?" Jessamy said, eyebrows raised.

Susan grinned. "Yes, but I had to play along and call him WG. I didn't think you'd bite my head off for it though, so that reaction was real."

"Thanks for your help, Ms. Hale," Griffin said, then he took Jessamy's hand. "If we're going to make the flight, I think we'd better high-tail it."

They barely made it to their gate and the gate agent closed the door of the jet way behind them.

When they were safely buckled into their seats in First Class, and the plane was taxiing to the runway, Griffin took her hand again and gazed into her eyes. "I love you, Jessamy Taylor."

"And I love you, Griffin Sanderson."

The kiss that sealed the deal was so sweet, Jessamy couldn't wait to get to their hotel in Miami.

A Note from Bev Elle

Thank you so much for reading **Fly Me to the Moon**. If you enjoyed it, please take a moment to leave a review at the retailer where you purchased in the USA, or other countries where it is on sale.

I enjoy hearing from readers. Please contact me via my website, where you can sign up for my newsletter to be notified of new releases, read my blog, and contact me via social media.

www.bevelle.wordpress.com

—Bev Elle

Newsletter: http://eepurl.com/3PosH

facebook.com/bev.elle.5

goodreads.com/bevelle

https://twitter.com/Bev_Elle

Authors With Similarly Themed Stories

Unscheduled Departure

by T.M. Franklin

Rowan Elliott is devastated when her boyfriend, Finn, tells her he's moving across the country to take over the family business, and thrilled when he changes his mind at the last minute and gets off the plane.

But then things get . . . weird. Finn's acting strange, and Ro's getting mysterious phone calls that have her questioning if her boyfriend's really who she thinks he is.   As Ro races to figure out what's going on, she discovers it's more complicated than she could have ever imagined.

And if she's not careful, she could lose her Finn forever.

Find out more at www.TMFranklin.com

Eye of the Storm

by Beth Bolden

Commercial pilot Captain Grant Montgomery III lives for the rules; flight attendant Tess O'Brien loves to break them.

Tess hates running into Captain Montgomery when she's working. On her best day, he's intimidating and kind of an ass. On her worst, he bore the brunt of the most embarrassing moment of her life. So when she's forced to drive from Columbus to Cleveland with him in the middle of the worst snowstorm Ohio's seen in years, Tess can't imagine anything more terrible.

But as they drive further into the storm and further into danger, Tess discovers that so many of the assumptions she'd made about Grant are flawed, exaggerated and even just plain wrong. She was hoping the trip would finally confirm once and for all that he's a jerk, but instead, she finds herself increasingly fascinated–and attracted–to him.

Discover more at www.bethbolden.com

The Friendly Skies

by Amanda Weaver

Cassie Sinclair has been there, done that, and has the frequent flyer miles to prove it. She's far too jaded to fall for the engaging stranger seated next to her on her flight to Mexico, no matter how pretty his face or dreamy his accent. But when the flight's re-routed and their tightly packed schedules are blown, she decides indulging in one reckless night with Simon couldn't hurt. They'll have their fun and fly back to their regularly scheduled lives the next day. But fate (and Simon) might have other plans.

Find Amanda Weaver at

http://www.amandaweavernovels.com/

A Midsummer Flight's Dream

By Kira A. Gold

Twenty years ago, on a quaint island off the coast of Sweden, a boy promised to catch Jolie if she fell from her aunt's roof. Now, her life has hit rock bottom, and she must fight her way through the airport security determined to impede her journey back to Öland, where she is met with new challenges, forgotten memories, and Mattias—now a successful and wealthy family man. Can Jolie rediscover who she is, and get home in one piece?

Contains young lust, old books, and wild strawberries.

For book news and other silliness, follow Kira on twitter: @KiraAGold

The Lost Queen

By Angel Lawson

When Liam Caldwell's plane makes an emergency landing at Nomad Airlines, Nadya is quick on the scene to help. Her family has run the airport for generations and Liam is one of their most important customers.

He's pulled from the plane bleeding and injured but no one, including her father, seems too concerned.   He disappears before 911 can show up, piquing Nadya interest, so much that she follows him home. This decision ignites a dormant connection between Nadya and Liam, one that spans from this world to another.

The Lost Queen is a four part series, by Angel Lawson. Find news and information @ www.angellawson.com

OTHER WORKS BY BEV ELLE

Upcoming Books From Bev Elle
The Parisian Assignation

Stephen has lived most of his life believing he was an unassuming Cranford, son of Anne, a housewife and Douglas, a local family practitioner. He has finished college, begun a career, and is engaged to a swimsuit model. What more could an All-American Boy ask for?

On his twenty-eighth birthday, Stephen learns he is the sole heir to the fortune of Étienne François Masson, the legendary philanthropist and CEO of Masson Enterprises. To claim his fortune, and guard it against a hostile takeover by his father's half-brother, he has to move to Paris to learn all the ins and outs of the empire his late father left him.

The company hires an assistant for him before he arrives, one who is fluent in both English and French, and is someone with whom he shares an intimate past—someone he'd sooner forget.

American born Nicole Parker has studied abroad since she was in grade school, and is an MBA and expert linguist. She is excellent at what she does, but for some reason she rubs Stephen Cranford, entirely the wrong way. Will this Parisian assignation prepare Stephen to be an international tycoon,

or will his assistant drive him to distraction, in more ways than one?

Coming in 2015!

Excerpt from The Parisian Assignation

Chapter 1

Stephen Cranford tried not to dwell on the fact that within the hour, he would meet and have dinner with one of the richest women in the world. However, it was all he could do not to salivate over the mere size and complexity of her portfolio; it was the wet dream of any broker worth his salt.

He loosened his tie as he left the Loop where he worked as an Executive Commodities Broker and maneuvered through the remnants of rush hour traffic in downtown Chicago. He wove through stalled lanes and bottlenecks in the same manner he traded on the Market, anticipating openings and making aggressive moves to claim them.

After another brutal day watching commodities do things they hadn't done since the big one day drop in 2008, he was ready for a gourmet meal and an expensive bottle of wine. The Dow was down more than 2000 points. Fears about the European sovereign debt crisis and the crumbling U.S. economy dominated the marketplace.

These events created fluctuations in the Market much like the death of billionaire Étienne François Masson had done earlier in the year, but that had been a cakewalk compared to current conditions. However, for Stephen, Masson's death had ranked in the league of a catastrophic event. The business tycoon had been his idol while in college.

Stephen would forever remember his location and what he'd been doing when he heard the news about Masson six months prior. He had been home, making love to Darcy, his fiancée, when a news bulletin interrupted his favorite jazz station.

Darcy had flown into Chicago for a photo shoot and declared it, in her own words, "Sex Sunday." She stripped upon arrival and they had spent the day christening various pieces of furniture in his condo. The woman was nymphomaniacal in her love of sex; who was he to complain? They worked each other over whenever she was in town, and their sexual gymnastics usually held him until she breezed through town again, invariably on the weekends.

He had Darcy bent over the chaise in his bedroom. She had orgasmed once already, and he worked at a frenetic pace toward his payoff when the music was interrupted.

"Billionaire Étienne François Masson, a French businessman best known as chairman and CEO of the French conglomerate Masson Enterprises, the largest luxury-products company in the world, has died at the age of fifty-four in a skiing accident at his resort in the Swiss Alps. According to Forbes Magazine, Masson was the world's fourth and Europe's richest person, with a 2011 net worth of forty-five billion dollars..." the radio announcer droned on about Masson and his accomplishments in life.

Stephen slowed his stroke and barked out a surprised exclamation. "Fuck me!"

"That's what I'm trying to do," Darcy gritted out through her panting, as he fell out of sync with her. "Move your ass, Cranford."

He'd felt her clench around him as hard as she could, like a reprimand. He reclaimed his rhythm, and in minutes had elicited another orgasm from her and found his own release. They collapsed in a heap on the chaise.

"You love me, don't you, baby?" she'd whispered, eyes vacant, her mind contained. She didn't expect a serious answer to her question which, in truth, was why their relationship worked.

She expected pithy, meaningless answers and he didn't disappoint. "More than a bull market." His heart was as inaccessible as her mind.

Within a minute or so, Darcy had exhausted her threshold for the obligatory cuddling after sex. When she began to squirm, he'd let her go. It was as if their roles were reversed in that respect.

The irony wasn't completely lost on him that he felt stronger about the death of a man he didn't know than for his and Darcy's relationship.

As fiancées went, she was perfect for him. She could have been high maintenance, but she was a fucking anomaly if he'd ever seen one. Darcy Vale was a supermodel whose face graced the pages of the world's biggest fashion magazines, but she worked all the damn time, traveling every week. That left him often to his own devices, which suited him just fine.

His engagement was as much a decision to yield to the status quo as an arrangement of convenience. He was twenty-nine and figured if he were to tie himself to anyone by the time he entered his thirties, Darcy would be the highest caliber of trophy wife he could get. There was no real love there, but she was gorgeous, a tigress in bed, and someone he didn't have to romance. She was busy, as was he, and her approach to their relationship was as practical as his own.

It was an arrangement Stephen was sure even Masson would have appreciated.

Stephen had often drawn parallels between Masson's personal life and his own. The man had gone through women like *they* were a commodity. Stephen had done the same years ago when the girl he'd considered the love of his life cheated on him. What past event in Masson's life had made him the kind of man he was?

While fascinated by the news about Masson, Stephen didn't harbor any ill will toward him like some undoubtedly did upon his death. In fact, he had rather enjoyed delving into Masson's business and life while researching his case study. Now though, it would seem that the man who had everything had died alone. Stephen would make damn sure that wasn't him in fifty years.

With her physical needs sated, and appeased by their pseudo-emotional exchange, Darcy had dashed for the shower. Stephen lounged on the bed and fired up his ever-present MacBook. Surely there was information about Masson's death on the internet. If anything could be categorized as such, this was *breaking news,* and it would profoundly affect his job at the Flagler Group in the short term and change market conditions in the long term. Masson Enterprises used any number of commodities and by-products in the manufacture of their luxury goods. Ripples from Masson's death would be felt through Exchanges around the world. He'd quickly read the front pages of several ISPs and the financial e-zines to which he subscribed.

Bemused, Stephen realized that though he was saddened by Masson's death, he'd been excited about how he'd clean up in the aftermath, so much so that he considered joining Darcy in the shower for a celebratory round. He knew she would want dinner, and dancing at a club. There was always later, after the club, and Darcy with a few drinks in her was a whole other phenomenon.

The memory of that day six months ago had come flooding back when he received a phone call from Madame Delphine Masson's personal assistant, requesting a meeting.

Stephen was glad he wasn't still working on the trading floor, because his conversations with clients, juggling of portfolios, and doing a half-assed job manning his own monitors were all a blur. He was also fortunate he hadn't worked on any discretionary accounts. Stephen could handle his more savvy clients' speculations and hedges with his eyes closed, but the phone call had robbed him of his focus.

It was rare he left work early, but curiosity about Madame Delphine Masson's request to meet had overtaken him, and he'd called it a day after putting in only nine hours, a record low for him. It was just as well; he had worked himself into a frenzy trying to figure out why *he* was summoned. Stephen would go just to see what she wanted, and how she had acquired his name. He didn't have to get involved in her "matter of a grave personal nature," as her employee had indicated earlier while making the appointment with him. What could it hurt?

~vPAv~

It was busy as Stephen entered Ria, The Elysian Hotel's Michelin two-star restaurant, but Madame Masson would have stood out in any crowd. Her regal confidence outshone the elegant simplicity of her attire. Stephen would guess she was dressed in the best that Masson Enterprises' designers had to offer. She sat on a chaise in the vestibule, flanked by two suits—presumably bodyguards, judging by the intelligence-grade earpieces they wore. It would have been foolhardy for a woman of her net worth to be in a foreign city left unguarded. She appeared comfortable and undisturbed by the obvious interest of the other patrons who looked on, wondering who this woman was.

Recognition sparked in her eyes, as well as another emotion that Stephen couldn't identify. Then, her stare became direct and blatant, her assessment bordering on rude. She was still a beautiful woman despite her advanced age. She stood with a warm smile as Stephen approached, grasped both his hands and squeezed them.

"Étienne, I am so glad you could join me," she said in perfect, albeit accented, English. She pronounced his name exactly as if she might have spoken to her own son. Stephen didn't correct her. She'd lost her son in a tragic accident. The least he could do was allow her that one indulgence.

While doing his case study, he'd found that Étienne was the French version of Stephen, which meant "crowned." He and the Madame's Étienne shared a similarity in their names, but that was where the comparisons ended. Masson might have been crowned prince of a business empire, but Stephen had just begun to embrace his potential as a businessman.

"Your invitation evoked equal parts honor and curiosity, I must admit," Stephen said with his own earnest, yet nervous, smile.

Who wouldn't want to meet the mother of one of the most accomplished and admired businessmen in the world?

"Please forgive me, I have a hard time with the name Stephen," she said.

"It's quite all right," he assured her.

The hostess approached, rescuing Stephen from the awkward greeting. "I see your dinner guest has arrived, Madame Masson. Your dining room is ready. Right this way."

Stephen stood aside and allowed Madame Masson to go before him as they followed the hostess through the restaurant to a private dining room. The hostess seated them at a table for twelve, but it appeared they would be the only two dining. The bodyguards remained outside the door.

Stephen noticed Madame Masson staring again, but this time her eyes glistened with what looked to be unshed tears. He wanted to ask if she were okay, but she spoke before he could form the words.

"I'm sure you must be thinking that this meeting has come from out of—what is that baseball term you Americans use?"

"Left field?" Stephen supplied.

"Exactly... " her voice was husky with emotion."I cannot believe that I allowed my husband to deprive me of this joy."

Madame Masson spoke in ambiguities but seemed harmless enough, so he would humor her in whatever purpose she had in mind. He'd get a fabulous meal from the type of restaurant he only patronized when he tried to impress a woman.

Perhaps sensing his unease, Madame Masson offered her assurance. "I promise, Étienne, I may be advanced in my years, but

I am in possession of all my faculties. We will come to the business of this meeting soon, but first, let us get to know one another, have a meal together and I will tell you why I have sought you out."

"I know it's after the fact, but my condolences on the passing of your son. He was brilliant, and the direction in which he moved the business was a true inspiration to me."

Her eyes misted, and she dabbed them with her napkin. "I wish my François would have had the opportunity to hear you say that."

Stephen felt like a cad for reminding her of her grief, but he wondered if they were speaking of the same man. "François?"

"Our family referred to my Étienne by his middle name," she explained.

"My apologies, Madame. I know his death must still be difficult for you. By today's standards, he was still a young man."

"*Oui.* A mother lives with the possibility that her child might precede her in death, but prays all the while that it will not be the case. I am thankful for the fifty-four wonderful years he was with me." She cleared her throat delicately and took a sip of water.

By the time they ordered, Stephen learned that Madame Masson had been born in Marseilles, and had met and married Nicholas François Masson when she was just seventeen. Nicholas had been fresh out of college and a lion ready to devour the world. His two companies and hers were the seeds that created the original conglomerate, but their son, François, was the mastermind behind Masson Enterprises as it existed today.

"What was your son really like?" Stephen asked as he tasted his first course, veal sweetbread *crosnes*. Madame Masson looked surprised, so he felt obliged to explain his interest. "I was somewhat of a huge fan in college. He was the subject of my graduate case study, but you can only get so much information from periodicals and the internet."

Madame Masson's eyes lit up in delight. "François was quite the precocious adolescent, but driven to achieve, and proved to be as shrewd a businessman as his father. He excelled in sports and was quite a passionate champion for the less fortunate. Later in life, he was branded as a fun-loving Casanova by the media, no matter how philanthropic and well-meaning he actually was. He lost someone very dear to him as a young man. I don't believe he ever got over her."

Stephen noted her discomfort and offered his empathy. "Things that happen in early relationships can definitely color a man's perspective."

"You speak as one who's lost in love? You're such a handsome young man, and quite charming. I can hardly believe that a young woman would be stupid enough to let you go." She took a sip of wine.

"Oh, you'd better believe it." Now it was his turn to be uncomfortable, so he changed the subject. "You have a daughter who heads one of the business groups, correct?"

"Yes, Nicoletta is Vice-President of the Wine and Spirits Business Group. The Lefevre Winery and French Hops Distillery was my dowry, so to speak. Nicoletta fell in love with the vineyards when she was in her teens. It's been her life's work. One of her sons has taken an interest in the business and will most likely succeed her."

"Has it always been so easy to get the younger generations to embrace the family business?"

Madame Masson laughed and lapsed into French. "*Non, mon cher...* ," then self-corrected. "My eldest granddaughter is married and has two young children and no head or desire for business. Thankfully, she married a young man who is a great provider. My grandson, Arnaud, who is about your age, used his trust fund to found a dot-com about five years ago." She rolled her eyes. "I do not see the appeal in managing a product that you cannot see, but he's doing well, so that should be all that matters, *n'est pas?*"

"Yes, it is." The waiter delivered their main course, and Stephen admired the dish Madame Masson had suggested for him. "So, how does the American offering of French cuisine compare to what you're accustomed to?"

Madame dabbed her mouth with her napkin and gave his question a bit of thought before she answered. "As a French restaurant on foreign soil, it is exceptional, but nothing compares to authentic French food prepared with love in one's own home."

"I feel exactly the same way about my mom's cooking. When I was away at Harvard and then Wharton, I missed it so much."

Her interest seemed piqued as he mentioned his mother. "What was it like for you growing up, Étienne?"

Stephen told her about growing up in Chicago, playing little league, polo, golf, and piano. Barely breaching the upper middle class, his parents were masters of living within their means. The only areas in which they'd splurged had been their children's educations, from elementary to post-secondary. They had all gone to private schools, which boasted the finest academic curriculums and extra-curricular activities available.

He swallowed a bite of sole. "I had a happy childhood as childhoods go. My parents always worked. My dad's a physician, and my mom taught Elementary School for a few years, until she realized she'd much rather write children's books so she could be home with her family. She was modestly successful at it, enough to gift each of us with trust funds when we came of age."

"Are your siblings as successful as you are?"

"Maybe moreso. My brother, Gavin, is a law partner in a relatively prestigious law firm here in town, married with two sons. My sister Elise, also married, has a son and daughter and manages the Arielle Chantilly boutique on the Magnificent Mile not far from this hotel."

"Ah, both great careers. Your sister has exquisite taste. Arielle Chantilly is one of our clothing lines." Madame Masson said with genuine interest.

"Yes, it was one of the lines added after I did my case study at Wharton."

"We acquired it about six years ago," she confirmed.

"My sister likes the changes that were made by your company."

"That's good to know." Madame Masson repositioned the napkin in her lap. "Are you not attached, Étienne? You didn't mention a significant other, or children. Only those of your siblings."

"As a matter of fact, I'm engaged to Darcy Vale, a model with whom you might be familiar. She's been on Masson Enterprises' payroll a time or two."

"Why, yes. She's been the face for our fragrance and jewelry lines. A beautiful girl that one, but she doesn't strike me as the type who would settle down, take care of a husband and have babies. But then, what do I know? I'm a septuagenarian, and this is the twenty-first century."

Stephen didn't know why, but that statement made him feel like he'd been scolded by his grandmother. In fact, Madame Masson reminded him of his dad's mother, grandma Kitty Cranford.

He indulged her with a smile. "Maybe we work because I'm not the type to settle down and be taken care of, and I like my nieces and nephews just fine, thank you very much." Stephen noted they'd been served a Lefevre Chardonnay, and held up his wine glass in a toast.

Madame Masson touched her glass with his and laughed a hearty laugh. "Touché."

Stephen did not refuse dessert. One thing about gourmet restaurants that he both loathed and loved was their serving sizes always left room for dessert.

"Now, to business," she said without ceremony. "I have a proposition

"I'm listening," he said with a smile. The excellent food and expensive wine had made him amenable. Besides, Madame Masson was a great hostess.

Madame Masson fixed her grey eyes on his. "I would like for you to come to the reading of my son's will in France next week. I believe I will be in a position to offer you an assignment in Paris that will begin the process of grooming you to replace François. I'd like to think that my Nicholas and François, were they alive, would approve of this move."

Stephen's jaw dropped. "I don't understand," he said. "I'm an Executive Commodities Broker, not a CEO."

"However, you have an undergraduate degree from Harvard and a Masters in Finance from Wharton. Not chopped liver by way of business degrees, as you Americans would say."

"Wait," he said, his brow furrowed. "Why would you want *me*, a virtual stranger, to attend the reading of your son's will and head up your company, for that matter?"

"Go talk to your mother and father, then come see me again," she said in a cryptic tone. "I'll be flying back to Paris on Sunday in the company jet. I'd like you to go with me. The will reading is next Wednesday. Once you've spoken with your parents, I hope you'll wish to communicate again. I'll let the desk know that you're expected."

Stephen fought hard not to frown in his increasing confusion. "Madame, I've been making decisions without my parents' blessing for a decade. Why is it so important for me to have their approval?"

"It's not their approval I'm asking you to seek as much as their disclosure."

He was slightly taken aback by her serious tone and smiled to soften his response. "So, my questions are to remain unanswered for now? That's hardly fair."

"What would not be fair is for me to tell you what only they have a right to. Go, talk to your parents, Étienne." There was a note of finality in her voice, and who was he to argue with a seventy-two-year-old billionaire?

Stephen couldn't wait to have that conversation with his parents. He was ready, if it would help him understand why Madame Masson had propositioned him to accept an assignment at Masson Enterprises. He let the top down on his car as he headed back to his condo, hoping the crisp Chicago night air would clear his head.

He'd heard the rumors after Masson passed away. The family was purported to have launched a search for a long lost heir to Étienne Masson's fortune—a love child he'd fathered by an American woman.

Fuck! Does Madame Masson think I'm the heir?

Surely not, he thought. He was Douglas and Anne's son. He had his mother's eyes and hair and was just as stubborn and meticulous as his father.

If he were Masson's biological son, his mother would have to have cheated on his father, because he was the youngest of the Cranford children. Anne Cranford didn't seem to be the type to cheat, but neither did someone else he'd known.

Stephen looked at his watch; it was ten o'clock and if he knew his parents, they weren't in bed yet. His dad was probably reading a medical journal while his mom was watching the news. He picked up his cell phone and hit their home number on speed dial. His mother answered.

"Mom?" Stephen called much as he had when he was a kid coming home to an afterschool snack; he half expected to hear the admonishment to get his homework done and practice piano before he went out to play.

He could hear the smile in his mother's voice. "Stephen, you've been too much of a stranger lately. I thought we were more important than that extremely expensive paper you peddle over at Flagler."

"You know you are. It's just—well—Darcy was in town over the weekend, and—"

"Enough said, son. You two don't get enough couple time. I don't know how you manage to keep a long distance relationship going, to tell you the truth."

"It's a challenge we're both up to, I guess. Hey, can I come by? I really need to talk to you and Dad about something."

Her voice was gentle. "You know you're always welcome to come home."

"Okay, see you in twenty minutes."

~vPAv~